The (D)Evolution of Us

Morwenna Blackwood

www.darkstroke.com

Discover us online:
www.darkstroke.com

Find us on instagram:
www.instagram.com/darkstrokebooks

Include **#darkstroke** in a photo of yourself
holding this book on Instagram and
something nice will happen.

To and because of,
Phil, Jenny, Mum and K.

About the Author

When Morwenna Blackwood was six years old, she got told off for filling a school exercise book with an endless story when she should have been listening to the teacher/eating her tea/colouring with her friends. The story was about a frog. It never did end; and Morwenna never looked back.

Born and raised in Devon, Morwenna suffered from severe OCD and depression, and spent her childhood and teens in libraries. She travelled about for a decade before returning to Devon. She now has an MA in Creative Writing from the University of Exeter, and lives with her husband, son and three cats in a cottage that Bilbo Baggins would be proud of. When she is not writing, she works for an animal rescue charity, or can be found down by the sea.

She often thinks about that frog.

Acknowledgements

In the same way that stories are inextricably linked, so I ought to thank everyone and everything that has touched my life, but here are a few special mentions.

Thanks to my family, especially Phil, for his unending love, support, encouragement and belief in me.

Massive thanks to Jenny and Alison from Imagine. I'm so grateful for the brilliant courses – especially the Novel In A Year course from which *The (D)Evolution of Us* was born – the writing days and events; for introducing me to the community of writers I now feel part of; for putting me in touch with Rob and Lee from Betterwrite, who have been integral to this process; for showing me what it really means to be a writer, and for generally being awesome!

I'd also like to thank all at my local Costa where *The (D)Evolution of Us* was written, as well as everyone at beautiful Northmoor.

I am indebted to our incredible NHS, and consider myself very lucky. Special thanks to those who've helped me over the years at TV, and S; and to Dr H for advising me regarding a medical query.

Thanks to Roland for being an inspiration and a fillip from so far away; and thanks to Karen for being my BF literally F!

Huge thanks to darkstroke for giving me this opportunity.

Finally, I'd like to thank Pandora for remembering to pack hope.

The
(D)Evolution
of Us

Prologue

Dear Dr Farefield,

I reviewed Catherine at The Meadows today. She reported that her OCD was less 'loud' than when we last met in November, after the Crisis Team was called. This improvement has coincided with the resuming of clomipramine, which seems likely to have been helpful, as it has been in the past. Catherine agreed to the suggestion that this dose be increased to 200mg: 100mg morning and evening.

Catherine is coping well with life and states that her relationship with Richard is good. However she refuses to tell him about restarting the clomipramine, which is of concern to me. She has also resumed her writing.

I again offered Catherine a course of CBT, but she was resolute that she found it 'useless'.

Catherine has now found employment in a health food shop but struggles with her OCD when closing down the tills and locking up at the end of the day, though she admits that she recognises that her rituals are entirely irrational.

Overall, in spite of her very significant persisting difficulties, I think that Catherine's life has improved with the reintroduction of clomipramine.

Yours sinc,
Dr E Whittle
Consultant Psychiatrist

PRIVATE AND CONFIDENTIAL

Dear Dr Farefield,

I met with Kayleigh at The Meadows this morning, where she revealed to me that she is in the first trimester of pregnancy. She had requested the appointment (we were not due to meet again for another six weeks), in order, primarily, to discuss her medication, with regards to her new condition.

I found the fact that she did this encouraging, as I did her general demeanour. She was casually, but neatly, dressed, maintained good eye-contact throughout our interview, and appeared to have a good understanding of her mental health, and how it could impact on her (unborn) child.

We decided together that it would be prudent for Kayleigh to remain taking her lithium for the duration of her pregnancy, with close monitoring from her midwife and the Perinatal Team.
In spite of Kayleigh's reports of having been 'stable' for the last few months, I have suggested that we meet at The Meadows every six weeks for the foreseeable future. I have also asked her to make an appointment for bloods to check her lithium levels as soon as possible – it is critical that she maintains a therapeutic dose.

Yours sinc,
Dr E Whittle
Consultant Psychiatrist

Richard

I'm half-listening to the radio, running a bath for my girlfriend, Cath. She's sitting on the toilet seat, staring at me. I'm standing in the doorway, staring at her. Then I start to laugh. They're playing that song by Marillion – *Kayleigh* – the one her hippy twat of a best mate likes to say she was named for, even though she's too bloody old. I say she's a hippy twat – I'd still shag her. She needs a good seeing to – and a good slap. She dots her 'i's with hearts, for fuck's sake! And then the phone rings. Bloody witches.

I was expecting Kayleigh to call. She always knows when Cath's in trouble, or upset, as Cath does her. Whenever the phone rings, and it's Kayleigh, Cath says, 'Oh, I was just thinking about you,' or, 'Oh, I was just about to call you,' and she isn't bullshitting, either. I know she's not. It's pretty fucking freaky.

"Hi, Rich. Sorry for calling at this time of night, but I'm worried about Cath. She said she was going to call me tonight and I haven't heard from her, and you know what she's like for planning." Kayleigh gives an unconvincing laugh. "Is she with you? Is she okay?"

"Yeah, she's here," I reply. "She got a bit pissed at the Riverboat tonight, and that on top of her meds, well, you know how she can get. She's running a bath now, trying to sober up." I stretch the phone's cord as far as I can into the bathroom and reach to turn the taps back on hard until the bath is full.

"Oh, okay," Kayleigh says, and I can hear the relief in her voice "But she can't keep getting like this, Rich. We'll have to do something - I don't know - maybe talk to her psychiatrist?"

I'm silent for a beat while I take this in. Then I casually say, "Yeah, maybe. I try to keep an eye on her when we're out, but she'll sneak off, or get a sly shot on the way back from the loos. You know what she's like."

"Yeah, I know." Kayleigh sighs. "Oh well, look after her tonight, Rich, and I'll see you soon, no doubt."

"Yeah, thanks, Kayleigh. See you later." I wait for her to hang up before throwing the handset into the hall.

I hadn't taken my eyes off Cath for a minute. She'd stopped crying, but she was pale, and her eyes were still red and swollen. 'Talk to her psychiatrist', Kayleigh had said. Cath was still seeing him, then, after she'd said to me that she'd discharged herself like I told her to. Stupid bitch. She's so weak I just want to smack some sense into her. And how dare she think she can lie to me and get away with it?

I smile at her. I know her OCD means she's suffering, sitting as she is on the lid of the toilet. I open my arms, inviting her for a cuddle. I even tilt my head to one side.

She's unsure.

"Come on, babe. I know it hurts you, sitting there. We'll get you clean, then we'll go to bed, yeah?"

Reluctantly she gets off the lid. Her hands haven't touched it, but she holds them away from her body anyway.

On go the waterworks. She hesitates by the sink, but lets herself fall into me instead, her hands still held out to the sides. Her head finds its usual spot between my chest and shoulder, and I move so that I can smell her hair. There's something to be said for this cleaning thing she has – at least she always smells nice. I inhale deeply, wrap my arms around her.

"I thought you discharged yourself weeks ago," I murmur, stroking her shoulders a bit too hard. Her body stiffens in my embrace, and I can't decide whether to carry this game on, or not.

I take another deep breath and decide I will. "Is that why you can't put your arms around me? Put your arms around me. It's okay. You won't kill me." I rub her back, then slide my hands down her arms, and interlace our fingers. She sobs,

6

tries to push me away. "Come on, babe, it's okay," I purr.

"No. I... can't!" She is sobbing, trying to unlock our fingers, wildly trying to get away from me now. We struggle for a few beats. Then I snap.

"Have a fucking bath then, if you feel so dirty!" I pick her up by her waist and throw her in like I'd throw a dead Christmas tree into a skip.

She loses it, she's hysterical. She's scrambling to pull herself out. We've only been together for about a year, but I know how she thinks - the bath water will be contaminated. "Stop fucking screaming, bitch! You'll have the neighbours up here in a minute!" I push her back into the water with all the force I can muster, holding her down with my right hand on her chest. The other is trying to open the bathroom cabinet. I stare into her eyes. She's too scared to scream now; thrashing, gasping, making it worse. I'm fumbling in the cabinet. Got it. Spare razor blade. Wrong hand, but too gone to care. Her hands are clawing my arm – she's scrabbling up – angle's not great but I know I'm going to do it – I'm almost coming – still staring in her crazed eyes – I grin – I slash at her throat –

Catherine's Novel

Sweat drips from the red ceiling, like drops from a leaking tap, frizzing our hair, pooling at the bottom of our backs, slowly soaking our jeans. We'll stink by the morning, all of us, here, crammed onto the tiny dance floor, jumping because those around us are jumping; in fact, at one point, I am sandwiched between two strangers and my feet don't touch the floor. The bass reverberates up our legs, our ears are ringing as we shout the lyrics we know so well back at the band. Warm lager sloshes from our plastic pint glasses, down our hands, making the floor sticky. Laughing, I drop mine. It is immediately stomped on, and it splits. It's hot in here, and it's an effort to breathe. Someone's cigarette brushes against my arm, so I automatically lick my finger and rub the red mark. Then I stop, because I like the way it looks.

Kayleigh

Liam is singing *Supersonic* in my headphones, and I turn the volume up as high as I can bear it. It's raining – it's always raining – and I'm walking back home from town, over the bridge, and I think I just felt my baby kick. I'm feeling more sub-atomic than supersonic right now, though, and I'm either one of those and pretty much nothing in between, and I'm having trouble making sense of anything, and I'd like to just up and leave, but I can't.

In this town, everywhere is within a half-hour walk, and pretty much everyone knows everyone else from school. It's a picture-postcard place, so the grockles think it's quaint and come here on their summer holidays. They don't see that everyone over the age of fourteen has a problem with alcohol, and they don't see the downside of knowing everyone, either, or, rather, everyone knowing you.

Rich is my best mate's boyfriend and, for some reason best known to himself, he actually decided to move here. I mean he was living somewhere else, and he decided to buy, yes, BUY, somewhere to live. Here!

Cath told me (Cath's my best mate) that his parents were dead so he'd been raised by his grandmother, but she was dead too now, and, wanting a fresh start, he'd got a job in Tesco, doing the fruit and veg and sometimes the checkouts, and had bought a maisonette just up from the Riverboat. The grockles flock to the Riverboat in the summer, seduced by its name and proximity to the river, only to be disappointed when they get there, because you can't actually see the river when you're in the pub, not even from the beer garden. You have to walk up the road and look over the bridge, and even then it isn't the prettiest river to look at, because of the

9

concrete flood defences. Anyway, Rich is a charmer, and he can talk the hind legs off a donkey, but he works hard, and he's pretty resourceful, so when the deputy at Tesco left, the manager just asked him if he wanted to step up – no interview, or anything.

Cath says that Rich loves having to wear a suit. He's that sort of bloke. She says he gets up at six o'clock in the morning and stands in the front room in his boxer shorts and socks, ironing his shirt and trousers, listening to the Chris Moyles Show. Sometimes I think he could be Chris Moyles' long-lost twin. Sorry, that's not a nice thing to say – I take that back. His hands aren't covered in dirt from lugging sacks of potatoes about and displaying the bananas anymore, but they're still rough and powerful. You can tell he hasn't always been an office bod.

Cath had met Rich in Tesco when he'd still been on the fruit and veg. She'd come in for a banana, a mainly-salad sandwich and a Diet Pepsi every weekday lunchtime. She has the same thing every day. That's just what she's like. And he'd always be there, checking his 'availability'. At that time, Cath was working as a receptionist for Land and Underhill, the solicitors who practise like they're still in Victorian times. Their building's in a massive terrace of massive old houses that stretches from the bridge all the way round and up to the main church. Cath's office was pretty much behind the door when you opened it, so sometimes clients came in and walked right past her and into the waiting room, so she would have to get up and jog after them in her heels, and get them to come back and sign in and that. She used to get really embarrassed about it. I used to wait for Cath to finish sometimes on a Friday, and I hated it in there. The floors were wooden, and slippery; the sound of your footsteps would echo. The walls were petrol blue, and as there was no window, it was oppressive. The waiting room would have given a lovely view on to the garden and the river but, for some reason, they'd had the window boarded up. The original Victorian features had been retained, probably due to the fact they operated like Mr Scrooge, and were too tight to modernise. An incredibly dusty chandelier hung from the high ceiling. Cath used to joke that a hundred generations of spider were crawling all over it, eating each other due to the lack of flies as a consequence of there being no window. No wonder she wanted to get out on her lunch break.

Anyway, one day she'd rushed into Tesco on her lunch hour, probably looking stressed, and Rich was there doing the bananas. He picked up a particularly curvy one and wore it as a smile. Cath had laughed, and he'd given her the banana – and he wrote his phone number on it with the permanent marker he was holding. I bet it never entered his mind that she wouldn't ring it.

They started off meeting a couple of times a week in the Riverboat. It made sense. It was near her work and near his house. Cath was still living with her parents. She'd taken a couple of years out before uni – she pretended she did it so she could save up some money, but I knew it was really because she wanted to be near Adam.

Adam was her first boyfriend and, if I'm honest, even though she's with Rich now, I don't think she'd ever got over him.

Cath had loved Adam from that first Saturday night when I'd dragged her away from her coursework after months of trying to persuade her to come out to the pub. They'd got together and gone out for a bit, but it got a bit fucked up, and Adam didn't dump her so much as start avoiding her. It was all I could do to stop her camping outside his flat permanently. Anyway, stuff happened, and he moved away but, like I said, I don't think she ever got over him.

And now Rich has asked Cath to move in with him, but she says she can't because of taking the years out to save up for uni. Also, even though they haven't been together that long – not in the grand scheme of things – Cath says he's on about getting married. It's all a bit weird, if you ask me.

Catherine's Novel

Enough time has passed that they think it's all over. I mean, the haircuts, the weight gain and loss, the drinking, the cutting. I even got a new boyfriend – Luke. He used to work in the Barge, but now he works in the café in town – the one I used to have to go to with my grandparents in the school holidays. Heath, my (ex?)-boyfriend, knew him, but I don't know how, because Luke wasn't from round here, so they weren't at school together. Everybody loves Luke. He charms the old people, flirts with the women (I know it's just to get them to buy stuff), and he's attracted a Saturday morning crowd of lads for a "fry-up after a Friday night". He's boosted business no end, and reckons he'll be promoted to manager soon.

Like I said earlier, Luke used to work in the Barge, and although I'd seen him when I was with Heath, I'd never really *seen* him. Then, one night, when I could actually face going out again after Heath went away, I went out with Lola, and we got pissed right up. I only remember things in patches, but I know we went to the loo in cubicles next door to each other, chatting away while on the toilet, and I was staring down at my knees, watching them go in and out, so I knew I was about to go off my head, and then when I pulled my jeans back up, my purse wasn't in my pocket, so we were running round the pub looking for it, and then this tall, muscly older bloke came up to me with it in his hand. He was laughing and smiling at me, and was looking at me like we'd met before, even when we hadn't, and I thought he was quite fit, and then I realised that it was Luke-from-behind-the-bar. His dark hair had been buzzed off, army-style, and he had a cigarette hanging out of his smiling mouth, presumably because he had a Bacardi Breezer in one hand, and my purse in the other.

"Thought because you'd lost this," he said, nodding to the hand that held my purse, "you'd need this," he said, indicating the bottle of alcopop.

"Thanks," I replied, reaching for my purse. "But I'm a cider-and-black girl, usually."

"Not tonight, you're not," he said. "Tonight you'll have ladies' drinks."

So I did. Then we're in the beer garden, me pressed up against a wall, getting off with each other. We've been together for a few months now, and everyone seems to think we're made for each other, that he's good for me.

All the while, my OCD is getting louder and louder, and no-one notices. How can they not notice?!

A few months go by, and now my parents are going to Luke's café every Saturday morning for breakfast. Tim, my big brother, is going out for drinks with him. Luke's even got me wearing skirts. And he's on about us moving in together. Mum's ecstatic about my improved choice of boyfriend, and she thinks that because I'm in skirts and drinking dainty drinks instead of pints, that I am cured. Dad still wants me to go to university, but he's allowed me to take another year out. Ostensibly I'm recovering and saving up some money to help with uni and, because of this, and the fact I've only ever got A grades, Manchester Uni are happy to defer. Dad thinks I should stay living with them, and maybe move up to Manchester with Luke next year. That way I can save loads of money, and then live in a nice quiet place with Luke, instead of a "grotty student house with a load of grotty students." Mum and Dad's hope is that Luke will look after me, and I won't be tempted by alcohol, or worse. They're so transparent.

"Luke's good for you, Kate. He's already talking about going up one weekend to look for a flat, and a job. That says a lot – he's willing to uproot himself so you can get your degree. Then you'll be able to get a good job and settle down, forget all the stuff that happened last year." I wonder who Mum is trying to convince. And this "good job" stuff is getting on my nerves.

"I want to be a writer, Mum."

"Yes, a journalist, like your brother. Once you've got your degree, you'll just walk into a job."

"No, Mum, I want to write books."

A laugh. A smile. She may as well ruffle my hair and pat me on the head.

"You can write whatever you like in your spare time, Kate. But you need to get a proper job. And to do that you need to go to university. We've talked about this."

Richard

"I think it's a good idea, Cath. Your Dad's right. If you get a degree, you can get a decent job, and it's only three years. Kayleigh can come up whenever. I'll be there. It's not like you're not going to know anyone. We'll get a flat together. You won't have to worry about living with a bunch of druggies and weirdos, and I've already asked at work, and they reckon I'll get a transfer easy. This town's full of wankers anyway, and, no offence, but it's not exactly like you've got loads of mates you're going to miss." I probably should have left the last bit out, but it is true. Now she's quiet – probably wondering whether to cry or not.

Suddenly she says, "My family is here. My LIFE is here! And I keep telling everyone, but nobody's listening – I want to be a writer! I don't need a degree for that, and I don't have to move to do it either. All I need is for people to let me sit down for five minutes and write!"

"Well fucking sit down and write, then!" I yell at her. Her chin is wobbling, her hands are in her hair. I just want to hit her. "I don't know what you do when you're round your folks', but when you're here, all you do is whine on about it and clean stuff up!"

"I've got OCD, Rich! I can't help it!" On go the waterworks. I snap.

"Oh poor, poor little Cath. So sad and troubled with her fucking perfect family and her fucking perfect life! I would have bitten off my right arm to go to university – didn't know that about me, did you? You think you're so hard-done-by, but you've got everything! EVERYTHING! What the FUCK have you got to be upset about?" I hiss the last bit, right in her blotchy, red face. I'm so angry I could crush her. I grab her shoulders and shake her until her teeth knock together. She goes limp and crumples up in a heap on the floor by my feet. She refuses to look at me, so I tip her chin up with my foot. I'm still wearing my steel toecaps from work. I could kick her in the face and snap her neck. Thinking better of it, I say, "Stop fucking sobbing! Your face is a mess." Tears are streaming down her cheeks, taking her mascara with them. Her nose is running, and she's just letting it. Disgusting. How can you be so uptight about mess, and let yourself get in a state like that? She closes her eyes.

"I'm sorry," I whisper, and I crouch down next to her.

I scoop Cath up in my arms, carry her upstairs to the bedroom and lie her on the bed she just made. I fetch her cleansing wipes from the bathroom, sit on the edge of the bed, and gently wipe her face. She opens her eyes and smiles. I smile back. Then she reaches over and pulls the rest of the duvet over her.

"What are you doing?" I ask.

"I'm tired. I'm going to sleep for a bit."

"I'll join you," I say, grinning.

"No, Rich, I really need to sleep."

"You 'really need to sleep'," I echo. "I've just done twelve hours at work, and in that time, you've had a shower and done a bit of housework. But you're the one who needs to sleep." I'm speaking very matter-of-factly, and I am calm. It's a statement. And yet, the fear's come back in her eyes. She's actually afraid of me.

"I'm sorry," she whispers, "I just get so tired. I think it's the pills." To be fair, she is actually having trouble keeping her eyes open, but this winds me up even more. "I just want to go to sleep," she says again. A grin spreads across my face as I think of all the things I could do next.

"You want to sleep, do you? I'll help you then."

I climb up onto the bed, next to her, straddle her and put my hands around her throat. She goes limp again. I take that as permission, and squeeze. She quickly goes red and kicks her legs. Her hands grab my forearms. She's not just mentally weak. Her eyes are bulging and she's trying to speak. It's all I can do not to press harder. Eventually she passes out. I let go. Red marks, but I don't think she'll bruise. I get off the bed, light a Marlboro, and pull up the sash window and lean out. It's still light. A group of young lads walk down the hill, shoving each other around, singing football songs. They're off down the Riverboat. That's not a bad idea. I finish the cigarette and spark up another. I'm halfway down it when the bed creeks.

Cath is sitting up. "I love you," she says.

Catherine's Novel

I don't remember ever not knowing Lola. She's my best friend, and pretty much always has been. We are very close. Sometimes when I'm thinking of Lola, the phone rings and it's her, and she always seems to know when there's something up with me, like cats do. That's why I indulge her when she goes all witchy – there seems to be a connection between us. I mean one beyond the realms of science, so maybe her theory about the world *is* right. Anyway.

When we were little girls, we used to pretend to be witches. We wrote spells, and made up rituals in our bedrooms on sleepovers, with the curtains open when the moon was full. We learnt about nature and made 'magic' potions out of rose petals and grass seeds mixed with water from puddles and gathered in marmalade jars. Or the rain drops on leaves, dripped into our palms. We hated it when our mothers said our hair was too long and cut it into mullets – we didn't want to look like everybody else because we knew we weren't like everybody else. When we were outside playing, Lola made daisy chains for our hair – I couldn't do it because I bit my nails, so I couldn't make the hole in the stems. Mum used to say that we looked like 'little hippies', but we felt the word 'witch' suited us better. Lola was the one who drove it all, but I kind of identified with it, so I went along with things.

Halloween was (obviously) our favourite time of year, and the Halloween of our thirteenth year was especially significant to us, because of the 'unlucky' number, and the fact we were now teenagers, and therefore in a new phase of our lives. We felt we should mark it with a ritual. That day didn't fall on a full moon, sadly, but a half-moon, and we made it special by saying that we were two halves of a whole. It was a Thursday, and I lied to my mum and dad and said I had after-school hockey practice, and so wouldn't be home till tea-time. Lola never felt she had to lie. She was always so much braver than me.

When we met in the playground after school, her eyes were already glazed. She told me to look in her rucksack. Wedged in with her school stuff was an empty bottle of Cinzano Rosso which she told me, giggling, she'd just downed, and half a bottle of red wine. She said she took them from her parents' drinks cabinet.

"Oh my God. Won't you get done?!" I giggled.

"No – I don't 'spect they'll even notice it's gone. The Cinzano's been in there for ages, and it's not like I nicked a full bottle of wine. Anyway, they were the only things they had that looks like blood." That made me feel a bit sick, but I smiled and didn't say anything.

We walked into town – or rather I did. Lola was stumbling a bit, and kept having to touch the buildings to keep her balance. We were heading for the only park that had a pond (we needed all four elements, and didn't want to just put some bottled water in a dish), and it was pretty much dark. Our route took us downhill and over the bridge, to the other side of town, which meant we had to go past the Barge. I felt nervous because some of our friends' brothers went there with their friends, and as soon as we got over the bridge, one of them who I didn't recognise, who was standing on the pavement with an empty pint glass, smoking, shouted, "Whoop! All right, Lola! You're looking gorgeous, as ever!"

Lola just laughed and called out, "Not so bad yourself!"

"Do you know him?" I asked her.

"No! But he's kind of good-looking" she said and blew him a kiss as we walked past. That was a bad move because he laughed and said, "See you boys later. Looks like I'm in here!" and he jogged up behind, pushed in between us, and put his arms round our shoulders.

Lola laughed. "You should be so lucky!" I kept my eyes on the pavement, but she was really flirting, and she must have looked at his crotch, because she then exclaimed, "Bloody hell. You ARE pleased to see me!"

The man laughed and said, "Well I am, but it's actually just my keys in my pocket. At the moment!" And he pulled the biggest bunch of keys I had ever seen, out of the front pocket of his jeans, and waved them at Lola.

"Is that a dinosaur?" Lola giggled as she flapped the keys out of her face.

"Ah, you noticed that, did you?" He laughed, going a bit red, but picking out the plastic keyring anyway. "It's a pterodactyl, so technically it's not a dinosaur. But I'll let it go!"

"Silly me. Of course it's not. The only dinosaur here is you!" teased Lola, and they bantered for a bit. She would have gone off with him if I hadn't been there, I know she would have, and I could feel him willing me to leave them alone, but I didn't know what to do or say, and I didn't want to walk back past the pub, so I just kept walking with them, staring ahead. Eventually I realised that they'd stopped talking, and that he was glaring at me. And then it all went wrong. His voice was suddenly really sharp and cold, and he said, "Who's your friend, Lola? Is she always this quiet?"

Lola had obviously felt the atmosphere change too, because she replied, "Yes, she's the sensible one." She gave a little laugh before saying, "Anyway, we're on our way home – hadn't you better get back to your mates?"

We were out of the town centre now, on the straight road that led to the park, through the beginnings of a residential area. The streetlights glowed orange in the puddles, and the cold wind made my teeth chatter. I kept my head down, wishing I could disappear. The rucksack on my back was getting uncomfortably heavy under the weight of his arm. Lola tried to shake him off again. "Look, we really need to go, so why don't you go back to the pub?"

"No chance! I'd rather spend the evening with you fine ladies. Unless you want to come back with me and have a few more – your mate looks like she needs to catch up! Hang on, what's that clinking in your bag?"

He stopped, pulling us back, and yanked the rucksack off Lola's shoulder. He found the wine.

"Oh yes!" he said, steering us into the park, heading across the football field towards the bushes that surrounded the pond – exactly where we'd planned to do our ritual.

The man was telling us about how he used to play football when he was younger, but Lola wasn't responding any more. We threw each other glances when we thought he wasn't looking. I saw that she was frightened now, which made me feel even worse. The man stopped under a tree, by the pond. It was almost pitch-black. I think it was then that we both knew what was going to happen. We couldn't think how to stop it, and I could feel it in the air that nothing we did would change anything – it was hopeless, inevitable. He threw down Lola's rucksack and pulled her coat off, an arm at a time, while she just stood there, trying not to cry, letting him. He dropped it down, did the same to me, then yanked our arms so that we fell down beside him. He opened the wine and took a swig straight out of the bottle, before thrusting it at Lola.

She shook her head. "Drink the fucking wine," he said, quietly. She did.

He offered me the bottle. I shook my head, my eyes still fixed on the wet ground, sobbing openly. He grabbed my face and tried to push the bottle between my lips. That's when Lola ran for it. She'd only run a few yards and was shouting for help when he caught her up, pulled her back to face him, and hit her. I should have run the other way then, but I saw Lola go down and I scrambled to my feet but hesitated before running to help her. Lola was completely still on the wet grass. It was too dark to see if her eyes were open. Then the man grabbed me from where I leaned over her, with both of his arms around my middle and dragged me back into the bushes. Lola remained motionless and silent and I did too, as he wrenched my jeans down and forced himself, by degrees, inside me. The shock of the pain - I thought I was going to die. I hoped I was going to die. And then, in the middle of it, he asked me where I'd got my ring. On autopilot, I told him.

I just lay there and told him. Then my face was buried in his stubbly neck, and I wondered if I was actually going to asphyxiate in the smell of his aftershave.

Kayleigh

My heart was in my mouth when I arrived at the flat, and I was struggling to breathe. Rich had called me. He was in bits. As I got to the insurance brokers that he lived above, I glanced up and saw him, head out of the window, smoking quietly. He was ashen. I didn't call to him – he hadn't seen me, and I thought that maybe he wouldn't want to be observed in the private moments between finding his girlfriend dead, and the rest of the world getting involved.

No-one I had ever known had died before, except my Nan when I was a little kid, but I'd heard about the eight stages of grief, and that the first stage was denial, but I still didn't expect to feel this. Cath wouldn't have cut her own wrists. She'd told me not long ago that she was having a 'blip', and I knew she could get down sometimes, but suicide? I'd known Cath all my life. It couldn't be true. I paused before knocking on the door. Some black paint flaked off. Rich looked down, nodded, and disappeared inside. A few moments later he opened the door for me, and I stepped softly into the entrance hall. It had been a balmy June day, and it was cooler inside than out.

"Hi," he whispered with a sad smile. I felt okay. It might have been shock, this denial, but I really expected Cath to come halfway down the stairs, pop her head round the banisters, and laugh at us for being so silly. In fact, as Rich and I searched each other's eyes, I thought we were both going to laugh.

"Are you okay?" I asked, stupidly. I didn't know what else to say. Rich did the smile again, dropped his gaze from my face to the pavement, and kicked at a cigarette butt that someone had dropped. "Where is she?" Another stupid question; after I'd uttered it, I was scared of the answer. It might be true, what he'd said. She might be in the hospital, in the morgue.

"Still in the bath," he said, his eyes fixed on the floor.

"What?! Hasn't the ambulance got here yet?" I started running up the bare, wooden stairs, to his maisonette, my habitual long skirt hampering my stride. What if I could save her? Dodging the spartan furniture, I hurried through the living room, past the sash window out of which Rich had just been smoking, up a shorter flight of stairs, down the hall and into the bathroom. I'd been aware of a smell as soon as I entered the flat but had been in too much of a hurry to process what it was. When I saw the bathroom, it was as if I'd run full pelt into a brick wall. I couldn't breathe, my hands flew to my mouth, my eyes began to stream, and I doubled over and was sick on the floorboards.

The bath was full nearly to the brim, and the water was red and translucent, like when you rinse a paint brush in a jam jar. The deeper into the water, the darker the red got. No, the thicker it got. It wasn't water, it was human. It was Cath. Her face, forearms and hands were grey – she'd got in the bath fully-clothed – and only the top of her head broke the surface of the water. Her long, mousy hair floated like seaweed. She would soon slide down and become completely submerged, and then she really would be dead. I had to get her out. I felt a rush of adrenalin and shoved off the hand Rich had just laid on my shoulder. Plunging my arms into the red, I hauled Cath out. She was so heavy. I dragged her, sopping, out of the bath, and cringed when her head banged on the floor. I listened for breath, and, none being evident, I started CPR. 'Started CPR' – I didn't know what the hell I was doing, just dredging my mind for the first-aid course I'd been made to go on at work. Should I do a rescue breath? Had she drowned before she'd bled out? Or should I try to stop the bleeding – was she still bleeding, or was the red running because she was wet? I couldn't believe that my best mate was dead.

"Where the fuck is the ambulance?" I screamed at Rich. He stood in the doorway, aghast. Then he shook his head.

"Kayleigh, she's gone," he said, quietly. I paid him no attention, carried on. "Kayleigh," he said again, louder, "She was cold when I found her." I glanced up at him, arms still pumping Cath's chest. His eyes were wet, and he was quiet and still. I heard the sirens in the distance. He knelt on the floor, on the other side of Cath's wet body, and put his hands on my shoulders. I knew he wanted me to look into his eyes, so I looked down, and searched Cath's open, staring eyes instead, and realised that she wasn't there. I made myself look at the long, deep, diagonal wounds on her forearms. For a moment, I was completely numb.

There was a bang on the door. Rich went downstairs to let the paramedics in.

Catherine's Novel

Heath is the only man I will ever love. I love him irrevocably. I would die without him. From the moment I saw him in the pub, I knew I was going to fall in love. Last night we were sat on the wall, just the two of us, in the beer garden of the Barge. He was off his head, and I was quite pissed on cider-and-black. It was late – nearly 11 o'clock – and I knew they'd be calling time soon, so I asked him again, "Am I staying at yours tonight?" He had his own place – he was five years older than me – so we could just be free. Honestly, I could kiss him all night. I had my arm around his shoulder blades, but his back was rigid. I desperately wanted him to lean into me or turn and kiss me. Instead he raised his head and looked at the bushes directly opposite us. He sparked up a Marlboro Light, from the silver and gold packet.

"Okay," he said, still staring into the bushes.

"I'll be back in a minute," I giggled, excited now. It must have started working! I'd made a love potion, brew, thing, on Monday night, and had sprinkled drops of it round my bedroom. I thought I'd sprinkle some round Heath's flat, too, but when I went round he wasn't in, and I didn't want to sprinkle it in his garden in case it went on to someone else, so as it was only oils and herbs, I thought I'd get him to drink some. Before Kayleigh and I went to the Barge on Saturday night, I'd put some of the liquid in a plastic freezer bag, which I'd hidden in my boot. When Heath had gone to the loo, I'd opened the freezer bag, and dipped my finger into the brew, I'd dropped as much as I could into his bottle of WKD, while I'd been alone. WKD is bright blue, and it was quite dim in the Barge, so I'd known Heath wouldn't notice – he'd been pretty pissed anyway – and when he'd come back, he'd downed the lot! Now we would always be together! I almost skipped down to the phone box with elation. I found 20p in my jeans pocket and dialled my parents' number. They'd still be up – Dad would be just arriving home from the pub him and his friends always go to in a village three miles away, with a big, greasy takeaway burger; Mum would be forcing herself to stay awake in case I wanted a lift home. Even if I hadn't been totally in love with Heath, I would have wanted to not go home – they'd all be sat in the front room drinking coffee, and the only things on the telly at that time on a Friday night would be *Newsnight,* which always put me on edge, or some crappy film full of explosions and sex, and I'd sit there wishing the ground would swallow me up.

When I returned, Heath was in the same place and position he had been in when I left, but there was a cigarette butt on the floor between his legs, and he was halfway through another. He smoked Marlboro Lights – everyone else smoked the Reds, and teased him for having girls' cigarettes, but I knew he did it because it was healthier. When I was with him in his car, he smoked with the window right down, not just open a crack like Mum did. I walked back up to him, jumped onto the wall beside him, and circled my arm around his shoulders again. I felt his body tense, but then he must have realised it was me, and relaxed a bit. He stubbed the cigarette out on the bricks between his legs, popped a strip of Orbit chewing gum in his mouth, and gave me his gorgeous, wonky smile. His tongue was still a bit blue from the WKD.

"Let's get an Aftershock before they call time," he said, and slid off the wall.

"Okay," I said with a laugh.

Heath grabbed my hand and pulled me back into the heaving pub. We had to push our way to the bar. A group of girls standing in a circle were taking up most of the space, shouting along to Alanis Morissette on the jukebox. Heath paused for a moment, then pushed right through the middle of them, singing the chorus at the top of his voice, not looking at any of them, but scanning for Luke, who was one of the barmen. He clocked his friend.

"Oi! Luke! Can we get two green Aftershocks, mate?"

Luke was quickly gathering all the empties off the bar. He turned his head towards Heath and said,

"Nah, sorry, mate. We called time about five minutes ago."

"Oh, come on mate! I'll shout you a KFC tomorrow! And anyway, you owe me – you sold me an off WKD earlier!"

Luke was a bit confused, but he apologised, and then grinned, grabbed the bottle of neon green liquid off the shelf behind him, and nodded Heath and me to the end of the bar. He poured three shots, keeping his hands below the bar, handed one to each of us, glanced over his shoulder, and said "Go!" and we downed our shots.

When I first started going out, I'd sip everything to see if I liked it, but I quickly learnt that it didn't matter whether you liked it or not – if you wanted to get drunk, you took whatever was going, as fast as possible. It didn't stop me shuddering involuntarily, though. Heath and Luke just looked at me and laughed.

"Hang around for a bit, mate," Luke said. Heath nodded and sparked up another Marlboro Light. He handed me someone else's half-drunk Smirnoff Ice from off a table.

"Lock-in," he said.

Kayleigh

It's three days after Cath's burial now and I am exhausted. I probably wouldn't have slept anyway, because it keeps hitting me that I won't see her again, but Liam is doing what they call 'cluster feeding', and I can't remember the last time I slept for more than an hour in one go. The service was held in the Chapel of Remembrance, in the grounds of the town's cemetery – Cath's parents wanted her to be whole, and as near to home as possible. I wondered if that was what Cath would have wanted. No-one found a Will, anyway, so it was a Christian funeral. Cath had always battled with herself for not believing in a Christian god – we worshipped the moon and the sun in our hearts – but I couldn't tell her parents, Steve and Debbie, that. I panicked a bit, because what if my politeness had sent Cath to the wrong plane?

I was sitting in the front row, next to Cath's mum, who was in bits. I tried to have a little joke, betting on who would run out of tissues first. I drew a weak and reluctant smile from Debbie and decided to stay quiet after that.

Rich, and Cath's brother, Tim, were the front two pallbearers. They held it together, but I could tell that Tim was on the edge. I got up and said a few words about Cath and me having been best friends literally all of our lives ... tragedy ... waste. The truth was, I wasn't really feeling it. It felt like I was watching it all on telly; like I didn't know these people, and hadn't known Cath. I was going through the motions, and I worried that I didn't sound sincere. I worried what people were thinking of me, as I stood there in my flowery maternity dress (I'd thought that once you'd given birth, you went back to your normal shape. I hadn't, and my maternity clothes were all I could fit into). I was unable to cry. I looked at Liam, who I'd left with Debbie while I said my bit. I'd disconnected. Cath lay cold in a horribly closed coffin to the left of me, my baby was furiously alive in the arms of my dead best friend's grieving mother. I hesitated, and, to my horror, realised that I was leaking milk. I knew I couldn't go on with this breastfeeding. I didn't care if it was 'the most natural thing in the world', as people kept telling me – it was gross. I pulled my black cardigan tight around me and looked out at the people I was addressing. All the seats were taken, but no-one had had to stand at the back. Cath had a close-ish family, and although she knew a lot of people, she had always been a bit weird. She wouldn't mind me saying that. She was always fine when she was with me, but I'd watched her flounder in conversation with others – especially potential boyfriends – a million times. I don't know if it was a lack of confidence or what, but she often literally didn't know what to say. Until she met Rich. I think her parents were hoping he'd ask her to marry him. He said a bit at the funeral too – all the usual stuff, and how talented Cath was, and how she was "within spitting distance" of submitting her novel for publication. His words, not mine, and certainly not Cath's. I sat back down and took Liam from Debbie. His light-blue baby grow was speckled with dark spots from her tears. Then they played *Linger* by the Cranberries. Rich had chosen it, asserting that it was Cath's favourite song. It wasn't. Her favourite song was and always had been *The Riddle*, by Nik Kershaw. She'd been obsessed with Nik Kershaw since 1984, but Rich had been going out with her for just over a year, so obviously he knew best. Apologies if I sound jealous. I'm all over the place at the moment, and I can't make sense of my feelings. It's probably the hormones. But something doesn't feel right. I've always thought Rich was okay, but when he threw dust and a white rose on Cath's coffin, it was like he was feeding the ducks. And the weather was wrong – it wasn't gloriously sunny, or stormy, it was just a flat grey day, with a bit of drizzle from time to time. Something had sucked the colour out of everything. Tim was crying openly now, his hand on a crumbling Debbie's shoulder, while Steve tried to support her, his face like a stone. I threw in the bouquet of wild flowers that I'd made and turned away. I hadn't needed any of my tissues.

Catherine's Novel

Luke must have loved me once, because he told me something he'd never told another person. But I know now, though, that he despises me, and my team of psychiatrists, psychologists and support workers. He despises my months off work, and my myriad pills – I've tried them all at one time or another, in various combinations. He hasn't needed any of it. He prides himself on being stronger than I am, despises the Crisis Team emergency card that I carry in my purse, despises my "weakness".

When he was old enough to speak, he'd asked his grandmother, Yvonne, why he didn't have a mummy and daddy, and she'd told him – not even gently – that his mummy had become very ill, had to go somewhere else to live, and wouldn't be coming back, and no-one knew who his daddy was. Luke's mum, Emma, had been young when she'd had him – still in her teens – and she'd been a tearaway, hanging out with her friends downtown after school, sitting on the benches that encircled the pretty trees, scratching her name into them with stones, smoking cigarettes stolen from her mother's handbag, chewing gum, and flicking it at the people passing by on their way home from work. She would have sex with the older boys who were just about able to be served in the off-licence and eventually got pregnant. She hadn't continued with her education, even though she'd been apparently brilliant at maths – she'd stayed living in her mother's house, with the intention of raising her baby. I've made it sound like it had all been okay – it hadn't. Emma had carried on seeing her friends, drinking and doing drugs while she was pregnant – even when she was sick. She'd lived as though she'd got fat, that was all, in spite of Yvonne's attempts to reason with her that she needed to look after herself for her baby's sake. By the time the baby was born, Yvonne had been desperate, and at her wits' end, and she'd rowed continually with her daughter; this usually resulted in Emma running out, and Yvonne was left looking after baby Luke.

In order to support them, with Emma's father gone, Yvonne had taken a part-time job as a weaver in the big factory that produced lots of different fabrics, in the centre of town. Her shift started at 5 a.m., so she would leave Emma and Luke asleep. Often, when she came home for lunch, she'd hear Luke crying, before she'd reached the front door. Inside, Emma would be drunk or stoned, sometimes with her friends. Sometimes Yvonne hadn't been able to go in for the second half of her shift – she'd attend to Luke, before kicking the youngsters out. With the house empty, tears would course down her face as she gave Luke his bottle. She cried out to her dead husband, and prayed to God for help.

Eventually they'd reached crisis point. Yvonne was walking home for her lunch break as usual, and heard Luke howling, from down the road, but this time there had been no accompanying rock music. She'd unlocked the door and raced upstairs. Luke had been on his back in the cot in Emma's room, screaming blue murder. In the cot with him was a shallow dish that had contained the milk that had since soaked into the blankets and Luke's baby grow, along with a hunk of bread, torn from the loaf, but also torn from its crust; the house had been empty.

Emma had arrived home to find a clean, fed, and sleeping Luke in his grandmother's arms. Yvonne had composed herself, and quietly told Emma to leave. "You are no daughter of mine," she'd said. Emma had hurled a barrage of abuse at her mother, before running upstairs and grabbing a bag, which she stuffed with the few clothes she had, along with the dog-tags Yvonne had given her, that had been her father's, from the War, and had run back out of the house, slamming the door behind her. Yvonne said that what really broke her heart that day, was that Emma hadn't even looked at Luke, let alone kissed him goodbye.

Yvonne hadn't seen her daughter again until nine years later, when she had found Emma slumped in the bandstand in the recreation ground, a hypodermic needle in her left forearm. She'd used her father's dog-tags as a tourniquet.

As for Luke's father, Emma had never told her mother his name, although there'd been a rumour going round the town. Apparently an older bloke had been bragging in the pub one night about having shagged her, and said she had lied that she was pregnant to get him to marry her. However, when Emma had become obviously pregnant, the bloke vehemently denied having said anything; no-one had believed it anyway – he was in his late thirties, while Emma had just turned sixteen. Nobody different had ever come round to see Emma during her pregnancy or after Luke was born. So far as Yvonne was concerned, Luke didn't have a father.

Yvonne had been there when Luke was born. Emma had gone into labour early, when she was out with her friends, and one of them had driven her to hospital. One of the midwives had called Yvonne, who'd been allowed to leave work to be with her daughter.

Yvonne had said she could hear Emma from outside the hospital. She'd hurried onto the ward to hold her daughter's hand and help her through, but Emma had told her to fuck off, and had turned her face away. The midwives had told Yvonne it would be best for her to wait outside, so she heard her daughter refuse the gas and air she was offered – Emma had screamed that she wanted to be sure that the baby was hers; she wanted to feel it come out of her. She'd said "it". There'd been a window at the end of the corridor where Yvonne sat, and she'd said she'd watched the light change while she listened to her daughter's screams, crying. She'd tried to go back in, but Emma had just yelled at her to fuck off again.

Darkness had fallen when Yvonne heard the midwife tell Emma to "stop making all that noise, and just push!" Emma had said she didn't want to push, that if she pushed, her body would split in two, and they'd both die.

And suddenly the screaming had stopped. A few minutes later, one of the midwives had come out and told Yvonne that Emma was asking for her. Yvonne had been hesitant, but she'd followed the midwife back onto the ward, and gently pulled the curtain aside. She'd told Luke that she'd cried out – Emma had been very pale, and there'd been so much blood. Emma had looked up from the baby that had just been placed in her arms, and had just said, "Sorry, Mum."

Yvonne had told Luke she'd been allowed to hold him while Emma had her bath. She said she'd smiled at him, rocked him, and told him over and over everything was going to be all right now.

Kayleigh

One in, one out, I've always said. I'm surprised my baby didn't come that night – the night Cath died. I can still smell her blood. I think I've gone a bit Cath's way - I've washed the insides of my nostrils with soap and sniffed Olbas Oil until my eyes are nearly bleeding, and I can still smell it. My baby, Liam, came a few days before the funeral, when I'd stopped spending all day crying, and had managed to do some cleaning – 'nesting' it's called, apparently. He began his emergence into the world while I was in the queue for the checkouts in Tesco, with a trolley full of nappies, tissues and sanitary towels. He started to come when I saw Adam leaving the store. I only saw the back of him, but I'd know Adam's walk anywhere. He'd had his hair cut – the sandy curls I remember buzzed off close to his head. I hadn't seen him for ages. Where had he been?

And then – ahhh! Major cramps really low in my groin. I was scared at first that my baby was coming, but then I thought it couldn't be contractions because the pain was too low down. Even so, it was so intense, when it came, that I asked if I could borrow the phone in Tesco. The manager was really nice, and even called a taxi to take me home when I'd got off the phone. The midwife I spoke to agreed the pain was too low down to be labour – it was probably another one of the myriad things a woman's body goes through when she's pregnant, things they never tell you about. I thought you just got fat, threw up and got a predilection for gherkins – so naïve! Anyway, the manager held my arm and helped me back down the stairs. He even waited outside Tesco with me and saw me into the taxi. The driver had put a bin bag on the seat in case it was actually labour, and my waters broke – he said he didn't want a mess in his car. I grimaced through the pain and thought how men had it so easy. I wriggled – it was all I could do to stay in the seat. There are double yellow lines on my street, so the taxi driver couldn't park outside my house, but luckily he managed to pull up in the side street by the church, under the beech tree. He just sat there while I manoeuvred myself out of the car, so I just threw a fiver at him, and slammed the door as hard as I could. "Where are you, Cath? Where are you, Mum?" I muttered, trying not to cry.

Waddling across the road, redundantly squeezing what I hoped was my pelvic floor, I made it to my front door. My 'flat' comprises the top two floors of a mid-terrace Victorian house. The guy who has the freehold is Will, an artist in his late thirties or early forties who lives on the ground floor. He's great, and pretty good-looking. I never know what colour his hair will be from one day to the next, and he has some cool tribal tattoos. Will's only got the one floor, but he gets the back garden. The front garden is typically Victorian – a little square of concrete with a low wall round it, to separate it from next door. When I moved in I asked Will if it was okay to put a couple of pot plants out there, to brighten it up, and so that the main focus when you walked up the road wasn't the wheelie bins. He was fine with that, but he keeps coming home pissed (he's a happy drunk, though, not a lairy one) and stubbing his rollies out in them, so they don't really bring as much civilised cheer to the entrance to our homes as I envisioned. The back garden, though, is all ferns and lush green shrubs, but at the top end are rambling roses, towering hollyhocks and lupins, forget-me-nots and ragged robins. I can see most of it from my bedroom window, and I just longed to be in it, in another world, away from this all-consuming pain. I was praying for Will to be in. He keeps himself to himself most of the time, but he's been great since I've been pregnant: checking up on me, asking how I am. He even left a basket of fruit outside my door and offered to cook me liver and onions (for the iron). I hadn't noticed his VW Polo by the church though, so I kind of knew he wasn't home. The pain came again, more intense this time. I let my bag fall to the floor, my hands pressed to the front door, my eyes squeezed shut.

"Kayleigh, are you okay?" My jaws still clenched with the pain, I glanced behind me and saw Rich on the pavement. I managed a smile but shook my head.

"Something's happening with my baby." I gave a weak, worried laugh. Rich was standing next to me now, his head resting like mine on the door's flaking black paint. He put a tentative hand on my shoulder.

"Is your bag packed?"

"What?" Some liquid just dropped out of me and splattered on the paving slabs. There were no better verbs to describe it.

"Nice!" Rich said. "Your hospital bag. I think your baby's coming, and I'm going to have to take you in!"

"What?! No, I've still got three weeks to go, and I just called the hospital and they said it couldn't be labour," I said, trying to convince myself. I felt in my handbag for my keys. Rich grabbed the bag and helped me inside and up the stairs. He'd been here a million times with Cath, so he started making a cup of tea while I rang the hospital again. I got as far as dialling the number before the pain brought me to the floor on all fours. When the midwife picked up, the crushing ache was worse than ever, and I let out a howl like a wounded animal. Immediately Rich ran back into the room.

"Jesus, Kayleigh! What do I do?" He looked around wildly, I suppose for clean towels and a basin of water. In spite of myself, I laughed, there on my hands and knees on the front room carpet. Rich laughed too. "Fuck. Stay there. I'll get some stuff for you." Unable to get up now, with my head on the floor, growling through my teeth, I let him. The midwife was asking me questions and I tried to concentrate.

"So you'll be on the labour ward," she said. I fought for control of my body as another contraction started. 'Contractions'. It had only ever been a word to me. Now I had a face for the name, I understood why people said, 'welcome to the club'. And my baby wasn't even here yet.

38

"Low risk," she said. That brought me back to the moment.

"No!" I shouted down the phone. "No, I'm bipolar and I've been on lithium throughout my pregnancy. I think I'm supposed to be monitored or something."

The midwife was telling me to calm down, that it was all okay. She said that my contractions seemed to be close together, that I should time them, and to get to hospital as quickly as I could. Rich came through the door with an overstuffed rucksack.

"Okay then," I said, breathless and fearful. "Bye." Some more water dropped out of me. I had lost control of my body. This wasn't happening like I thought it would. "Let's go," I said to Rich. I missed Cath so much I started to cry.

Catherine's Novel

Princess Diana died last night. When I got in this morning – about eight o'clock – Mum and Dad were watching the telly. We don't usually have the telly on in the mornings – Dad likes to go up the little shop and get the papers, while Mum puts the kettle on and starts peeling the veg for lunch. Then he reads the paper while she goes through the magazines. I don't know why we get the *Daily Mail* – it's right-wing, and the magazine is full of expensive stuff. Also, the recipes in there are for people who have all day and no children, Mum says, and the crossword is too hard. I only read it for the horoscopes. Today, though, the news is on, and will be all day.

Princess Di was killed, in a car crash in Paris, with Dodi Al Fayed. People are putting bouquets on the railings outside Buckingham Palace. Mum is crying, which makes me start crying again – I've been crying all the way home from Heath's, but no-one has noticed that anything is wrong with me. I'm invisible. I make a cup of tea for us all, because that's what we do in our family – as if the tea will make everything better. My head is fuzzy and my digestive system is fucked. I had to go to the toilet at Heath's before I left – I mean really go. I rubbed some of his toothpaste on my teeth and swilled some water around my mouth, but it still tastes foul. I washed my face, but it's all messed up again from crying. More than anything, though, I feel ashamed, hollow and heartbroken.

We all sit and watch telly for a bit until Dad gets restless and says he's going for the papers. I ask if I can go with him – I don't feel so bad when I'm moving. In the car Dad puts the radio on. When Mum's in the car without Dad, she switches it off – she's never really liked music. I just can't stand all the talking. Today, though, there's no talking – just funeral music. Britain is in mourning, and I am too – but for a different reason.

I don't even know what happened between us last night. All I know is that I got paralytic. I somehow pissed off Heath, and I woke up in my clothes, alone on the rug in his bedroom. I didn't know what the time was, but I waited for ages for him to come back. I knew something was really wrong, and I was really scared, so I tidied his room up, put the washed dishes that were on the draining board away, and drank some water. He must have gone back to someone else's house – but then how did I get in? The people who lived in the rest of the house, who rented out the top floor to Heath, weren't about either, so, reluctantly, I used the bathroom, let myself out, and walked home.

All the way home I whispered 'sorry, sorry, sorry'. I even prayed to God to let it be okay. And I tried to replay the night, in my head. We had a lock-in, did a couple of Aftershocks, and I was also on the Hooch, but I don't remember us arguing, or if I did something, or what. I instinctively knew that our relationship was over, but I don't think Heath actually ever said the words.

Which means that if it's meant to be, it'll be, even if we're like thirty or something. And that's when I heard it again – the Universe talking to me. I knew it on a primal level. It said, "If you cut your hair, there's still hope." So I did.

Kayleigh

There was a note, but it didn't sound like Cath, that was the trouble. She was meticulous – she never would have written her last words on the back of a lottery ticket. More to the point, she was a writer (or would have been) and would have written an eloquent piece articulating her reasons for her decision, what was going on in her head, how sorry she was to everyone. Because she must have been sorry, mustn't she? She must have known how her death would affect us in ordinary circumstances, let alone taking her own life. And she probably would have been planning what she would say for months and bought some special paper and a fountain pen.

I picked up the pink ticket again, turning it over to look at the numbers – in case of what? In case there was a special code in them? When we were kids, we'd communicate in codes – using symbols for the letters of the alphabet, or sometimes using the number of the letter's position in the alphabet. There was nothing special in the numbers that I could see. I wondered if she'd bought the ticket, or if it was Rich's. Then I wondered if it was a winning one, and if we should check. What kind of a person thinks that? I quickly turned it back over again and read Cath's scrawled-in-Biro note:

I can't do this anymore

The e of 'anymore' was smudged by water. She must have written it while she was in the bath, unless the smudging had been from her tears. I imagined her, desperate, pulling out whatever she'd had in the pockets of her jeans that she could write on (her pockets were always full of 'important' bits of paper), then sitting, fully-clothed, in the water and slashing her wrists – bish, bash, bosh – before she had time to think better of it.

My instinct was to keep the note, but something had made me return it to Rich, telling him that he should give it to the police, who were, at that time, still taking photos in the bathroom. I wondered why they were doing that if it was obviously suicide.

Rich has been amazing. He stayed with me for the whole birth, encouraging me to take the gas-and-air tube, to breathe, and finally to push. I thought I was conscious and sober all the time, and I remember shouting that the gas and air wasn't doing anything, but I must have lost it for a bit, because when I looked down between my legs, a nurse was sewing me up. Where was my baby? And why was it so quiet? On the telly, the woman screams, the baby comes out, the baby cries, and everyone tells you how well you've done. A group of doctors were huddling in a corner to my left, and Rich was with them. I started to panic and cry.

"Where's my baby? Why isn't my baby crying?" I was just lying there, my feet still in the stirrups, blood everywhere.

Rich rushed over to me and held my sticky, bloody hand. "It's okay," he said. "He's just a bit sleepy – it might be because of your tablets. He's okay. They're just checking him."

"Him," I said, and smiled. Before I'd had time to properly register that he knew about my tablets, and wonder how, the nurse said, "All done!" She unclipped my feet from the stirrups. Instinctively, I moved a bit, finding that my legs had turned to jelly, and it was carnage between them. I pulled myself up a bit, and a load of gore came out. I realised that for the first time in months, I didn't itch, and I had no pain. I started laughing. Then I started crying. The midwife brought my little boy to me, wrapped in a clean, white towel. She placed him in my arms, and I realised I didn't know how to hold him. I cried a bit more. For weeks I'd been trying to think of something profound to say in this moment – my first words to my baby outside my belly – but all I said was,

43

"Hiya," and I kissed his tiny, delicate head.

Rich, with incredible foresight, had brought a camera, and he took a photo of me and my baby, and then of the midwife. She told him to stand next to me by the bed, and before I could think about what she was doing, she'd taken a photo of me, the baby, and Rich. A family.

I was relieved that my little boy, Liam, was a boy. If he'd been a girl, I would have had to call him Catherine, literally for everybody, and that would have broken me. As it was, it was okay, and Liam was Liam.

My Dad had moved to France with his second wife, by this point, and Mum had moved back up north where she grew up, so neither of them were about on the day Liam entered the world. I called Mum from the hospital payphone in the morning. She was beyond excited, and said she'd ask her work for a half-day and come down on the afternoon train. It was Friday, so they probably wouldn't mind – half of them went for a liquid lunch on Fridays and were useless all afternoon, like a load of schoolchildren – and she'd try to get the next week off so she could stay with me and help, for which I was eternally grateful.

Mum and Dad split up when I was thirteen (you couldn't make it up), and I still think it was my fault. I know that psychologically it's a classic reaction for a child to blame themselves when their parents split up, but I think there's something in it in my case. I started nicking stuff I thought they wouldn't notice from the smelly cupboard where they kept all their alcohol, and hanging around downtown in the evenings. I got off with some older lads who went to youth club. It was fun. It was an escape.

Cath and I had been doing what we liked to call Wicca since we were little. I can't remember how and exactly when it started. Anyway, it stuck with us, and when we were thirteen, we decided to do a ritual in the park that Halloween. The night before, when my parents were in bed, I went downstairs and nicked a couple of bottles of red wine from their cupboard. It had to be red, obviously. I'd intended to share it with Cath when we got to the park, but then I thought she'd be too square to drink much, so I necked some in the toilets after the last bell had rung. I thought I was going to be sick, but I kept it down. Then I met Cath by the gates. We headed for the park, which meant walking through town, and walking past the busiest pub, the Riverboat. It had a reputation, and we always said we'd go there when we were older.

There were some lads standing outside, drinking and smoking, and some of them wolf-whistled at us. Then one of them started following us, and hugging me, and I know I flirted with him a bit – because, why not? – and other than it being a cold and wet night, I can't remember anything else except waking up in the morning on my parents' sofa with a bloody great bruise on the side of my head.

I presumed that I'd fallen over because I was so pissed, and I felt bad because I don't know if I walked home with Cath or not, but she never said a word about that night, which was weird because it was supposed to be an important ritual bonding thing for us. And then I wondered if I had gone all intense, or just been too pissed, and had ruined it somehow? And I felt so bad that I never had the courage to bring it up, and then life went on, as it does, and eventually I just forgot about it. But I do know that afterwards – not immediately, but afterwards – we both started "going a bit weird", as Mum put it. Our parents rationalised our behaviour as a teenage phase. I'd always been a bit hyper, so no-one worried too much about me – I didn't get my diagnosis till years later, after an incident at school – but Cath kind of folded in on herself: she was never the same.

They (whoever 'they' are) passed Cath's death off as suicide. I think that I am the only person who didn't breathe a sigh of relief. No-one has to think they were to blame – Cath was ill, and she died because of it. If people worry that they should have treated her better, or whatever, that's in their own heads and no-one is outwardly holding them accountable. The inner world doesn't count, which is why mental illness isn't treated in the same way as a physical one. Anyway, to me, there's something really wrong about Cath's 'suicide'. I know, knew, Cath better than anyone, and I just don't think she'd have done it. She always said there was enough tragedy in the world, without adding to it. I remember when she was given a drug – Seroxat – one of the side-effects of which was suicidal thoughts – we laughed at the irony that an antidepressant could cause you to become suicidal – and she said she'd never do it because it'd kill her mum and dad; I mean, even when she was low as fuck, she was constantly aware of how it was affecting her family. And me. It felt like it was me and her against the world.

Rich and I were talking the other night. He's been coming round a lot, and I feel a bit dodgy about it, to be honest, but he's quite, well, maybe it's my post-partum hormones, but he's been so helpful with Liam, going shopping for me, cleaning up and that. He stayed over the other night – on the sofa – shit, of course on the sofa! Anyway, he stayed over one night, and we had pizza and a couple of cans of Carling once Liam was asleep, and he, Rich, actually got up when Liam woke up crying at two in the morning, and made me a coffee and put the nappy in the bin outside. He's been really nice, and he's funny, and I kind of see why Cath liked him. Okay, yes, it crossed my mind to ask him back into bed with me when Liam had settled. How fucked up is that? My dead best friend's boyfriend; my dead best friend's would-have-been-fiancé.

Rich says I'm in denial, that I'm not accepting that Cath was so messed up that she killed herself. But I *know* there's more to it.

Mum's eventually arrived. I don't know what happened to getting that afternoon and the following week off work. She never said. Liam is a month old now, and I think he thinks that Rich is his dad. Rich is here most days for varying periods, and he's usually brought a takeaway or some shopping or something. He's stayed over the last couple of weekends too. He's just been really supportive. Maybe this is how he was with Cath.

I had to stop breast feeding. I can't cope with it. It's supposed to be the most natural thing in the world, but it just feels wrong to me. I didn't realise it would hurt, for one thing, and I didn't realise that it can be difficult to do. Liam gets upset because he can't latch on sometimes – or, I can't get him to latch on, which is more like it – and then we're both crying. I don't understand it, because it was fine the first time I fed him. The health visitor has tried to help, but I think it's to do with something in me. I think of what my breasts have been for so far, all the boyfriends, and then, ugh, I just can't reconcile it with my baby. It's a real head-fuck. Lucy from the Perinatal Team said that sometimes what is "best for Mum, is best for Baby", so I've admitted defeat and got Liam on the bottle, which is great in a way, because it also means that I can drink alcohol again.

I tried to joke with Lucy over that, but she just sighed and told me something I'd been told before – that I "should avoid alcohol as it exacerbates the symptoms of bipolar disorder", and that it would interfere with my meds. She also asked me if I thought it was wise to drink when I was a new mother – she didn't voice 'single' between 'new' and 'mother', but we both knew it was there.

We – when did Rich and I become a 'we'? – have had to buy a steriliser and bottles, and a massive box of powdered milk – it's as big as my box of Persil – so my already cluttered kitchen is even more of a nightmare. I don't know if it's because he spent so much time with Cath, but Rich is forever putting things away, or at least trying to, which is a pain because then I can't find them. There's not nearly enough storage space for the size of the kitchen, but I fell in love with this flat for its big, airy rooms and high ceilings; not to mention the view of Will's garden. If I'm banging on about my flat, it's because I don't want to part with it, and I'm getting attacked on all sides. Mum says it's too close to the pub, and in an area that can't exactly be described as salubrious. Rich says I could save loads of money and have much more support if I move in with him, which I think is more than a little insensitive, since I'd have to wash in the same bath that my best friend died in. In fact, I think it's more than a little weird that he can carry on living there. If it were me, I'd have moved out the night Cath died and hired a professional removals firm to get all of my stuff out. Also, Cath died violently, and I'll bet anything that her spirit is still there. Maybe I ought to go round and try and talk with her. And finally there's Will. He really doesn't like Rich. Will's never been 'off' with Rich, or said stuff behind his back, but he's frosty with him, and defensive – Rich really gets his back up. Which worries me, because Will's got his head screwed on – he's eternally sensible and level-headed, and he likes everyone (except Rich), and everyone (except Rich) likes him. I don't know what the problem is. Dad – when I get to speak with him – says I'm "hormonal and paranoid", and I should just concentrate on raising Liam and forget about all these "bloody blokes". He's probably right, which is why I've made no changes, and also why I'm glad Mum's arrived – it means that Rich can't stay over and fuck with my head; he's been so kind to me, helping me with Liam and everything – just having someone else in the flat is a comfort – someone to find it funny when Liam pisses in my face when I'm changing his nappy sometimes, and to help me bathe him when he's been head-to-toe in a leaky poo, and to wash bottles and stick the steriliser on at three in the morning when I realise there won't be any clean ones for the morning (whatever that is, now) – I don't know that I could have done this on my own – and no-one else has been there for me – Mum's only just got here now, Dad's not even said that he's even thinking of coming to meet his grandson, and my bloody supposed-best friend has topped herself when she knows I need her most – and is it weird that Cath's almost-fiancé is kind of being a father to my son? Or is he the perfect person to be doing it? I'm surprised that Will hasn't made more of an effort – given how he's been with me in the past. Maybe Dad's right and I should just get a grip. Maybe I am hormonal and paranoid. And sleep deprived.

Richard

Am I fucking invisible? It's like I'm Clark Kent or
something. I'd thought for a while Kayleigh's niceness was a
front, and she was secretly turned on by the fact she was
shacked up with her best friend's ... me. But I think the truth
is that she's just a slut. I don't know whether I'm going to
burst into hysterical laughter, or if I'm relieved. Yes I do,
now I'm here, sitting on her loo seat staring at the back of the
closed door. I'm actually stuffing my jumper sleeves in my
mouth to stifle my laughter. What a silly bitch! She's got that
God-awful black and white poster of some muscled model
with his shirt off holding a baby, on the back of her bathroom
door. Christ, I bet she sits here every day, gawping at him
while she pisses, wishing he was her kid's dad. Him, or that
Gallagher twat. It's so typical of her to name her first-born
son after some indie northerner. I don't know how people can
stand to listen to that whiney guitar crap. I'm going to try to
get her into Old Skool so I can hear some decent music when
I'm with her. Which is nearly all my waking hours. I'm going
to make her wish I was the kid's father. And let's face it, I've
done more for her and her kid than that sperm-donor ever
did. Whoever he was.

I thought that when Cath had gone, things would have
balanced themselves out. I took the ring off her finger when I
found her – well, once the shock had worn off a bit – but my
fingers got all bloody, so I washed them a few times. While I
was doing that, I got distracted and I left the damned thing on
the side of the sink, where Kayleigh found it when she went
to wash *her* hands, and I bet she wondered why it was there,
because Cath never took it off. So now Kayleigh's got the

bloody thing hanging on a chain round her neck.

I have no picture of my mother's face in my mind, but do I have one of the ugly ring she always wore. It was a chunky, silver pentagram – totally plain, no stone, just metal – and it lived on her left hand as if she was married. I don't know how I remember it – I was still a baby when she abandoned me for her druggy mates – but when I saw it on Cath's finger that Halloween years go, the memory smacked me in the face like a wrecking ball, and I ended up doing what I did.

I spoke to Nan about my mother's ring the next day – just casually, just popped in for a cup of tea – and she said that when Emma had died, she, Nan, took the ring off her finger because she hadn't wanted her daughter to go to hell. Worried that she'd be cursed by it or something, she'd dropped it into her cardigan pocket while she worked out how best to dispose of it, and of course, when she went to find it again, it wasn't there. Nan said she'd been relieved because it solved her problem for her – the Lord moving in mysterious ways, and all that crap.

That Halloween, I'd been a bit pissed, and when I saw Kayleigh walking down over the bridge, I thought I'd try it on with her. I knew she was young, but she was fit as fuck, all dressed in black, and I overheard some bloke who was standing behind me saying that she had a bit of a reputation, and that made my mind up. I started up some banter, and she played along, so I thought I was in there. All I had to do was get her po-faced mate to fuck off, and I'd have a quick shag to make up for a pretty shit day. They both had their rucksacks slung over their left shoulders, and Kayleigh's mate was holding onto the strap of hers with her left hand. And that's when I saw my mother's ring. It was on her middle finger – she must have had smaller hands than Emma. And something in me snapped.

It was like my brain had disconnected. I was enraged – I mean literally. I had to destroy this girl. The fact that she was so submissive made me hate her more – at least Kayleigh had tried to run off. I grabbed Cath round the waist, pulled her back into the bushes, threw her onto her back, and pulled her

50

jeans down. The grass was damp, and I was aware that my knees were cold, and my jeans were now stained. I'd been drinking, though. I could always say I'd fallen over; the lads would call me a twat, and laugh, and that would be that. And halfway through, I put my mouth right on her left ear, and hissed down it, "Where did you get that ring?"

She was sobbing a bit, but she managed to reply, "Kayleigh gave it to me, so I'd know everything was going to be all right."

The Lord moves in mysterious ways.

And that's exactly how Nan would have accounted for me meeting Cath in the first place. However I prefer to say that it was 'Fate'. Fate, that I was in that town, in that pub, on that Halloween evening. Fate, that Kayleigh had a reputation; Fate that a random bloke made a comment about her within earshot of me; Fate that I heard her name correctly (if I'd have confused it with 'Hayley', the outcome might have been very different), and had the balls to call out to her. Fate, that the pub had been so rammed that I'd had to come out for some air at the exact moment Kayleigh and Cath were walking by. The whole thing is SO random, it HAD to be design. And no, I don't hold myself responsible for what happened. It was meant to happen. It was Fate.

Nan had lived in that godforsaken town her whole life, and it had been where my godforsaking mother had been born and raised. If Emma hadn't have died there, I reckon Nan would have raised me there, too. As it was, Emma overdosed, and Nan was so distraught that she moved away, taking me with her. When I was young, she used to say that she'd never set foot in that town again; but as I got older, and it was becoming clear that I was ready to find a place of my own, Nan decided to move back. She had a close friend there, she said, and that time had healed her. I helped her to organise and move to a bungalow on an old-people's estate, and that Halloween afternoon I had moved her in. It had been a bloody nightmare from start to finish, with the autumn weather, and the amount of crap she had, and the fact that I was the only one doing the lifting and driving. So I told her I

51

was going out for some beers and I'd kip on her floor for the night if I had to – which is exactly what I did.

When I'd finished with Cath, I stood up and pulled my jeans back over my buttocks. It was more like I'd just had a piss than just come. I'd looked around absently, but it was almost pitch-black in that part of the park. On autopilot, I'd sparked up a cigarette. The tiny, orange flame didn't make much of an impression on the darkness, but it did illuminate Cath. She hadn't moved. She was lying there on the cold, wet grass, naked from her waist to midway down her calves. I hadn't been able – or bothered, if truth be told – to try to get her jeans over her DMs, or to try to pull the bloody boots off. If she hadn't been sobbing, Cath would have been completely motionless. She saw me looking at her, and her eyes showed her fear. She reminded me of a dog that was waiting for the next kick from its owner. The spectacle repulsed me. I spat in her face and sauntered off.

I wasn't even worried. I knew she wouldn't tell. I went back to the Riverboat and had another pint, but I was overwhelmed by the feeling that I was worth more than this – watching these sad twats laughing at each other and getting off with each other, and pretending to have a good time, so I walked out, went to the offy, got a bottle of Mad Dog, and went back to Nan's. In the morning I drove home, and didn't think any more about it.

When Nan died, and I decided to move back to the place of my birth, I got a job in Tesco, and bought my maisonette so easily that it must have been fated. I used Land and Underhill as my solicitors, so I'd seen Cath there – she was their receptionist. She was pretty non-descript, so I barely acknowledged her. I was on the fruit and veg at Tesco to start with, and I'd seen her come in and pick up a banana for lunch every weekday, in the absent sort of way you get to know people by sight. One day I was hanging up the bananas on their hooks at the top of the display when she came in, and she reached quite close to me to pick a specific one with her left hand. And I saw the ring, and nearly fell off my kick-stool in shock. I looked at her properly for the first time and realised that she was the solicitors' receptionist. It was SO funny! She was still wearing the bloody ring! She caught me smiling and flashed me a quick, shy smile, out of politeness, in return – obviously unaware as to who I was – and walked off to the checkouts. And that was that. The next day she came in, I gave her my phone number, and waited for her call.

There are no coincidences.

Kayleigh

I almost forgot my next appointment with Dr Whittle. We'd arranged it back along, so we could sort out my Care Plan, and talk about making an 'advance statement'. In spite of everything, I was feeling okay. Liam was having a good day, so I was relaxed – for me – in the waiting room and was wondering if I really needed to make one. The idea was that if I was ever incapable of making decisions about my care, this statement would come into play, and things would be arranged according to my wishes – like a fucked-up Will. Basically, if I ever lost the plot again, things would be in place for Liam – I think that was the idea. I'd said at the beginning that my mum would look after him if I couldn't. Sometimes it felt like since I'd had my diagnosis, nobody ever really trusted me again.

Anyway, I was waiting on one of the green chairs, holding Liam, who was drifting off to sleep again, when Dr Whittle walked out of the department and straight past me. He looked a bit agitated, but then he had an important job. I smiled at him. It was about ten minutes before my appointment, so I thought he must have been dashing out to grab a coffee, or speak to someone quickly, or something. But when the clock got to 2 p.m., he hadn't returned. And then this guy in a full suit with a turquoise paisley waistcoat opened the door to the department and called me in. I was a bit confused, but I followed him anyway.

He led me into room four – Dr Whittle's office. The first thing I noticed was that Dr Whittle's plastic cactus wasn't there. The suited bloke leaned back in a higher chair than the one I was in, crossed his legs and arms, and smiled – but with just his mouth. Something about him made me look down at

Liam, and that's where my gaze stayed for most of the meeting.

"Hello, Kayleigh-Amanda. I'm Dr Grosvenor. I'm afraid that Dr Whittle has become unavailable for the foreseeable future, and I have been charged with the task of looking after his patients. I mean that I am your – *the* –" he corrected himself, "new Consultant Psychiatrist." He wiggled the foot of his right leg, and I could see the sheen on his shoe catch the light from the window.

I didn't know why, but I was afraid of this Dr Grosvenor. It wasn't dislike, or that he creeped me out. I was actually afraid of him. I stared at Liam who was shifting in his sleep, and I could tell that he was about to wake up and grizzle.

There was an uncomfortably long pause, then, "So how are you, Kayleigh?" Another pause, then, "How are you coping with your baby?"

Involuntarily, I hugged Liam even closer to me, which woke him, and he began to cry. I tried to meet Dr Grosvenor's eyes, but his glasses acted like lasers, and I couldn't hold his gaze. Just being in his presence drained me.

"Kayleigh, I asked you how you are. How are you coping with your disorder, now that you are a mother?"

I got really confused and wasn't sure what I should say. I asked what had happened to Dr Whittle.

"Dr Whittle is unavailable for the foreseeable future, as I said, Kayleigh, and I'd appreciate it if you would answer my questions. I have read through your notes, but I need to assess your current state for myself in order to –"

Liam was really distressed now, and I stood up and started rocking with him. Suddenly I knew what was wrong. This man was a psychic vampire!

"I'm a what, Kayleigh?" Dr Grosvenor said, leaning forwards.

"Nothing! I'm doing fine – we're both fine! My baby is upset – I have to go now." And I left him sitting there, his glasses and his shoes shining in the autumn sun.

Cath's mum phoned me up that evening after I met Dr Grosvenor. Liam had fallen asleep on his bottle, his long, almost translucent eyelashes casting a shadow on his perfect cheek, so I put him in his Moses basket, and was curled up on the sofa with Rich, watching *This Life.* We were sharing a bottle of cab sav – the first proper alcohol I'd drunk since falling pregnant (I wasn't counting the couple of Carlings we had the other day) – and I bloody needed it after my meeting with Dr Grosvenor. I felt a bit spaced out as I walked into the hall to answer the phone. Debs, Cath's mum, asked me to go round to theirs and help her go through some of Cath's more personal stuff – diaries and things. She said that though it broke her heart sorting out Cath's clothes, she felt okay doing that, but that it didn't feel like a mother's place to read and keep or destroy Cath's private writings. I was so not in the right head space for that conversation, especially not at that time of night. Debs was still grieving hard. She didn't sound like herself. She sounded distant and uncertain, and like she was about to burst into tears. She probably was – she'd lost her daughter – and here I was, just a handful of months down the line, cuddling up with the man that we all thought Cath was going to marry.

"Who was that on the phone?" Rich asked when I sat back down next to him on the flowery patterned sofa. His demeanour had changed completely, and I was suddenly scared.

"It was Debs – Cath's mum. She wants me to go round and have a look through some of Cath's stuff –"

"Why just you?" he snapped. "Why hasn't she asked me to go round? I am – was – her boyfriend!" He sounded really defensive. I suppose he felt left out.

"I don't know. I wasn't really thinking, what with the wine, and you being here and everything."

"Why shouldn't I be here?" He was sitting bolt upright now, his gaze hard. "I really like you, Kayleigh, and we all need to move on." I didn't have time to make sense of what he meant by that – in fact I think he was surprised that it had come out of his mouth – because he quickly went back to his

56

first question: "Why didn't Debs ask me to help? Do you think she doesn't trust me?" He looked pale now, and scared rather than angry. Why would he be scared? I wondered if he'd seen Cath's ghost in his flat.

"What? Why wouldn't Debs trust you? She wanted you and Cath to get married – remember?! I think you're being paranoid. Here, have a top up –" I leaned over him to reach the bottle that was in the middle of the coffee table in front of us, but he flung my arm away, so I fell back against the sofa, then he jumped up like I'd just gone to stab him or something.

"Fuck off, calling me paranoid! I never laid a finger on Cath! And you're the one who's schizo, not me!"

"I never said you did anything to Cath, Rich. Where the hell has that come from? And what do you mean I'm 'schizo?'" I was perched on the edge of the cushion now. I cursed myself for drinking so much wine – I couldn't make sense of what was happening.

"You know damned well what I mean. You're on lithium because you're so fucked up. Debbie know that, does she? Eh? That her dead daughter's best friend is a psycho?"

Richard

They're all the same, sharing their secrets with each other, leaving me on the outside, huddling round their cauldrons, whispering. I'm Cath's boyfriend, for fuck's sake, and if anyone should be able to look through Cath's stuff, it's me. I gave her jewellery for her birthday and Christmas and that, so I should be able to take it back. I've got nothing of hers to keep – not that I want anything to keep – I'm on to the next one now – but I think everyone's forgotten that I've lost a girlfriend. I deserve the special treatment more than anyone, but I still get up and go to work every morning! People are so self-indulgent.

If I'm honest, though, there's more to it than that. Cath wrote things down. I know she kept a diary, and I knew she was writing a novel. It didn't interest me much at the time, other than that if she finished it and if it was good, it might make her a packet, which would obviously be good for me. I could kick myself that I never took a look at it. I never read a damned word!

Now she's dead, of course they're going to look through her stuff, especially because it was suicide. Everyone's looking to see if she wrote anything that shed a light on her mental state. And here's the big question - did she write anything about me, and how I was with her sometimes? I could always say she made it up, but would they believe me? I mean, she wanted to be a writer after all, and there's no proof. I never left a mark on her, but I'm nervous. If they look through her diaries, ten-to-one I'm in serious trouble.

Catherine's Novel

Honestly I could scream! No-one is listening to me! I don't want to go to fucking university! I don't need to! Why is everyone pushing me? Do they want me to spend my entire life sitting exams? Or do they just want to get rid of me? Am I that bad a daughter? I know I get drunk a lot, but that's only to escape my head. It's not like I'm on drugs or anything.

I'm in the town centre, sitting on a wooden bench under the weathered statue of some important bloke. I've lived here all my life, but I've never known who he was or what he did. Time has rendered his name unreadable; I trace a finger over the smooth indentations as if some psychic connection could be formed. I'll go to the library later and look him up. That's the only reason I can see for going to uni – they'll have a much better library than the one here. I can imagine myself cold, in a library that's like a cathedral, curled up in a corner where two bookshelves meet, in fingerless woollen gloves and a long scarf, scribbling something. I'd love that, if I could escape from this world and be completely absorbed in a different one, oblivious to time passing. Then, when one of the librarians comes and tells me they're locking up for the night, I'd get the bus home and grab whatever food I'd have in the cupboard – food would just be fuel – and read and write until I fall asleep. I could do that till I die. But if I move away, Heath won't know where to find me. I have to stay here to keep the connection alive – the Universe is telling me to.

Kayleigh

Damn it! How did Rich find out that I'm bipolar? I've kept it hidden from everyone except Cath and my mum and dad, for years. It's not that I'm ashamed of it, but Rich's reaction said it all – people think you should be locked up. I know that patients aren't systematically sectioned any more, but pretty much everyone thinks that every mental illness is the same, and that you're insane and dangerous. Or that you go running to the doctor for Prozac whenever you feel a bit sad. To be honest, I didn't realise that there was a grey area until I was told I was in one.

Rich stormed out of my flat after his outburst, and after the shock wore off, I became aware I missed him. Even when he was asleep, night feeds didn't feel so lonely and helpless. It's two-thirty in the morning, and it's totally black outside. Liam has fallen asleep in my arms halfway through his bottle. It was dark by half past four this afternoon, after a dank day of never-ending drizzle and low cloud; it was just cold enough to make you miserable, without being cold enough to make you hope for snow. The wind's got up now, and I can hear it throwing rain at the windows. I asked Will if there was any chance of getting double glazing this year – in answer, he wondered which of us was going to win the lottery, laughed, and walked off.

Halloween has been and gone. I'd carved two pumpkins that day – one for Liam and one for Cath – and put them on the coffee table. I'd pushed the table up against the window so they could be seen from outside. When Rich had gone that night – he said he was meeting some mates down the Riverboat – I got my old witch's hat out and sat there with a cup of green tea, the lights off and the curtains open, watching the candles flicker in the pumpkins, the rain running down the window panes, the people off to the pub, or taking their kids trick-or-treating. 'I'll be joining them with Liam in a couple of years,' I thought. Then I'd cried. Halloween has always been sacred to me.

I shake myself out of my reverie and look over at the pumpkins, which are still on the coffee table, even though I've moved it back. They're beginning to rot now. I take the dead tea-light candles out and put them in the bin. Amazing what you can do with one hand, when you have a baby. It feels wrong to chuck the pumpkins in after them, but what else am I going to do with them? "Merry meet and merry part and merry meet again," I murmur, thinking of Cath. The pumpkins fall apart when they hit the bottom of the bin.

Catherine's Novel

Every year, on September the first, Mum and I stand outside the patio doors in the morning and look at the garden. One of us always says something along the lines of, "I can feel September in the air." Except this year I've been feeling a chill from the middle of August, and have been coming downstairs in my dressing gown. I've got a pair of woolly socks over my normal socks, too. Dad's slurping his cornflakes in his armchair, watching the news. He tells Mum, who's already standing outside, to slide the door closed a bit because he can smell her cigarette. He nods and grunts at me – at least he's acknowledging my presence. I pad over to the patio doors and smile at Mum. She's taking hurried puffs of her cigarette, brushing some fallen ash off her tights.

"You're running late," I comment.

"I know. I've got to take the minutes today, and I need something to calm me down. There was dew on the grass this morning, when I came down to make a cup of tea – September's in the air."

"I know. Funny how the season changes just like that. I don't know if it's because of the schools going back or what, but September always feels more like a new beginning than New Year does."

"I don't see the point in celebrating the New Year, anyway," says Mum. "Your dad likes it though. And next year it will be a new start for you, too. You know I bought you that dressing gown to take to university, don't you?"

One of them was bound to say something. I should be halfway up the M5 on the way to Manchester right now. Instead I'm at home, not even dressed at seven in the morning, going to work to stack shelves soon. I can see where they're coming from – "My daughter stacks shelves in a health food shop" doesn't sound as good as "My daughter's at university in Manchester". But if I don't stay here, how will Heath know where to find me? The more I think of it, the more obvious it gets – if he'd wanted things to be over between us, he'd have said so. He's probably just mulling things over. I've read that men tend to retreat when they're in a quandary. Maybe that's what Heath's done. Maybe this is a test, and he wants to see if I really do love him. Last night, down at the Barge with Lola, I burnt an H into my arm with my cigarette, dragging the burning tip along my skin. Lola didn't notice – she was too busy getting off with this blond bloke who was wearing a fur-lined jacket, outside the toilets. My arm still hurts a bit, and it's very red – another reason for wearing my university dressing gown.

Last night, me and Lola were standing by the wall in the beer garden, and we'd had a few white-wine-and-lemonades (Lola was trying to look a bit more classy, and I think Luke's ideas were beginning to rub off on me), and I was telling her about my writing and how I don't need a degree to do it and that, and she said that Barney (the bloke in the furry jacket who she'd been getting off with) was at Exeter Uni, doing "English or writing or something", and he'd been banging on about a bloke called Frank Kafta (or something like that) and had I heard of him? I've heard the name, but maybe I need to read up a bit, just in case I do go at some point. I could hang out at the library on my days off. Yes! Why didn't I think of this before? Then I won't have to be at home, washing things and feeling guilty for not having gone to uni. And the library's just up from the Barge, so I can walk past and see if Heath's there –

"Kate!" I snap back into the present, slightly dazed. "Kate, I'm off to work. Don't you be late either – you're doing this job to save up for university. Don't forget." Mum smiles as she reaches the end of her sentence to soften it, but her eyes are sad. Worried.

Half an hour later and Dad's gone to work, dropping my brother, Tim, off at his work on the way. I am alone in the house. The patio door's still open. Damn! There's no way I'm just going to be able to shut it, lock it, and go. The tears that are perennially behind my eyes drop down my cheeks, and I can smell that smell that seems to be permanently in my nostrils. I drop to my knees, put my head in my hands, and watch the tears make their dark circles on my dressing gown. After what seems like eons I get up off the floor and punch my legs to get the blood back into them. I slide the door closed, pull up the handle, and turn the key. I walk away, up the stairs, and into the bathroom. I shower for ages. Mum's constantly moaning that I use up all the soap. I think of Lady Macbeth – 'Out, damned spot.'

I can't help but shake the bottles of pills as I put them on the shelves. I hate my job, but I feel okay here – safe, and there's no pressure. My manager, Tasha, is always on about how if people only ate properly they'd feel so much better, and there'd be no need to be on the Pill and take Prozac. I got a bit paranoid the first time she said it, but eventually realised she wasn't talking about me, just people in general.

"All the Prozac-poppers could just take St John's wort instead - it's a flower, for God's sake, it's pure and it doesn't fuck up your body. And the girls could just take evening primrose, if they need anything. I think people think that PMT is an illness, but it's not, it's just the female body trying to do what it was designed to do. People seem to think that everything should be perfect all the time, and by 'perfect' I mean that things should be exactly how they want them to be, but life's not like that." She flips her hennaed hair dismissively, and I wonder where her opinion comes from.

As I watch Tasha step down off her soapbox, I notice Barney, ostensibly looking at the range of herbal teas, but he's smirking to himself. He quickly turns to face me and raises and drops his eyebrows. He's holding the ginseng blend, but I know he's going to be on the Aftershocks again later. I flash him a quick smile and carry on with my stacking.

Tasha is saying something else, but I miss it. Has Lola told Barney about me?

"Kate, are you there?" Tasha's big moon face is close to mine. She uses Kingfisher toothpaste, and a herbal antiperspirant that she must know doesn't work. Lola's going a bit that way – all hippy – but I need the chemicals to scarify me. Lola gave me an old ring for my thirteenth birthday – a silver pentagram – to remind me of the Goddess, and the beauty and goodness in the world, and that all we need can be found in nature. I wear it because she gave it to me, so I can be reminded of her. I rub the ring and send up a prayer for Heath.

Luke is expecting me to call in and see him on my lunch break. I have to go in and buy the same thing for lunch every time, to keep Heath in my life – the Universe tells me to. If Luke knew that, he'd kill me. I'm stacking the St John's wort now, which is a relief as it's on an eye-level shelf, so I don't have to stretch, or stand on a kick-stool. My horrible work-shoes are rubbing my feet, so I'll pick up some plasters from Tesco later, too. I ponder taking St John's Wort, but you can't take it if you're on antidepressants, and I need to at least give them a go. I need something to help me deal with kissing Luke, when I should be kissing Heath. I keep rubbing my ring when my hands are behind Luke's back, so that the Universe knows that I'm true to Heath and am only kissing Luke as a survival tactic. It occurs to me that Lola never said where she got the ring, although she'd said it wasn't new.

Richard

I got Kayleigh pissed up on red wine last night. I was staying over at hers again, and I offered to do the night feeds or whatever, so she could have a drink and not worry about Liam. He pretty much sleeps through the night anyway. He's a laid-back little kid, thank God. I want to know who his father is. Part of me needs to find out so I can find the bastard and kick his head in. In spite of myself, Kayleigh's all right and, as kids go, so is Liam. It pisses me off that I'm doing all this for him and getting none of the credit for it. It pisses me off that he's not mine. I've never bothered with condoms, and somehow I've not got a kid. Not that I know of. No-one from the CSA has come after me anyway. I bet some little bitch is keeping a secret from me, somewhere. They're all the same, with their bloody secrets. Unless I'm not meant to breed – maybe the world wants my mother's fuckwit genes out of existence. Anyway, most of me just wants to know who Liam's father is because Kayleigh's so bloody secretive about it. I thought the wine would make her open up, but after I'd asked a few times who the father was, she just snapped and said, "It's not important! Liam's got me, and that's all he needs." And she got up and went to the loo, and when she returned, she put that bloody Oasis album on, and started talking about how she could do with a night out at the Cave, or whatever that bloody shithole of a club is called. But I'll find out sooner or later. When she falls asleep, I'll go through her stuff. And I'll try to get that bloody ring and chain off her neck as well.

Kayleigh

Rich wasn't happy when I told him my mum was coming down. He shot me a dark look. For all he's been doing for me, he can still be scary when things don't go his way. I actually thought about doing a protection ritual. I wonder if Cath ever saw that side of him – she never said anything. No – I'm probably paranoid – she can't have, or she wouldn't have been thinking of marrying him.

It's early – only just light – and Liam's been up and wide awake since four a.m. I'm pushing him around town in his pram, trying to get him off to sleep again. He's tired, I know he is. I've wrapped him up warm in the little rainbow jumper Cath's mum gave him. Town is so peaceful right now. The leaves are warming to look at, with their fiery colours, and the lights from some of the windows of the flats above the shops make me feel fuzzy inside. I love the promise of morning – a new start for everyone. I push Liam's pram through the piles of fallen leaves, and kick them up with my feet, so that he can hear them. I can't wait till we can do this together. I imagine him doing that cute run that toddlers do, and jumping in the puddles. We're heading home now, past the town hall, past Rich's flat on the other side of the road. I stop on the bridge to show Liam the ducks and swans, but he's asleep now. I have to keep pushing the pram – it's the motion that has lulled him – so I walk straight past the Riverboat, avoiding a plastic container on the pavement and the chips that have spilled out of it, and straight past our flat. I know where I'm going. We're going for a walk in the park.

There are no streetlights in the park. That's one of the reasons Cath and I chose to do our ritual there all those years ago – to be able to see the moon better. Now, early on a November morning, I can see just about well enough, and some of the orange glow from the street filters through the semi-naked trees. Liam is still asleep and I feel okay. What am I expecting? We've been in the park hundreds of times since that weird Halloween. Today though, I push the pram to where I haven't been since that night – up the twisting little path that leads to the pond. There are more fallen leaves here than in the rest of the park, because this path hardly ever gets used. It's been raining, so the leaves are slippery too. The pond is dark and is still partially covered in algae. I reach into the side pocket of my bag and find a coin. I drop it into the pond for luck. It sinks with a thick plop.

I look around. The park is empty, bar us. I glance down at a sleeping Liam. His little knotted hat has come down over his eyebrows, so I gently push it back up his forehead. He stirs but doesn't wake. Leaving the pram where it is, I step off the path and onto the wet grass. I unclasp the chain from around my neck and let it dangle, the weight of Cath's ring moving it back and forth. I touch the ring to the ground, and turn on the spot, making a circle. I kick my black DMs off so that they fall near the pram. I feel more connected to the earth in bare feet, and I peel off my now wet and muddy socks. I'm not quite sure what I'm doing – I haven't done this for years – and then something makes me look up.

In front of me is a gnarly old tree, and leaning up against it is a man. He's staring at me. It hits me that Liam is crying hard, and suddenly I'm scared. I dash to the pram and run with it as fast as I can over the grass and tarmac in my bare feet, desperate to get away. There are footsteps gaining on me, splashing over the wet grass, then slapping on the path. I am crying too now and can hardly see. I have to get my baby somewhere safe. Breathlessly, I call to Liam that it's all right, trying to convince both of us. Then I realise that someone is calling my name. Without slowing down – we're nearly at the park gates – I look over my shoulder. The man is only yards behind me. "Kayleigh! What are you doing?!" I'm still running, but I'm confused. I know the voice. "Kayleigh!

68

Stop! What the fuck are you doing?!" I look around again, and then I stop running, and start crying. It's Rich. Relief floods my body, and I nearly collapse into him, but I have to hold Liam, who is still crying, so I scoop him out of the pram, blankets tangled and dangling from his legs. He is purple, and fat tears bead his cheeks. I hold him tightly and kiss his head. Rich's arm is around my shoulder, his hand bent up to pull my head into his. A noise escapes my lips – relief, exhaustion. My body automatically starts rocking to soothe Liam. The three of us rock on the leaf-strewn path, like a family reunited after years apart. Rich drops my boots and socks, and tries to stroke my hair, but it's too tangled. Liam is quiet. I let my head relax into Rich's shoulder. Our eyes meet, and we start to laugh. And then, for no apparent reason, I am suddenly scared again.

Catherine's Novel

Life was a lot clearer when I was young. The older I get, the messier and more opaque it becomes. I remember spending evenings after school, the bit between tea and bed, in the park, sitting at the top of the climbing frame with Lola. We'd tell each other our secrets – who we fancied, who we hated, that we'd smoked a cigarette, or knew what a condom was – while we swung on the bars and tried to scratch our names into the flaking paintwork. One day, Lola was doing rolls over the top bars, over and over, and she said she'd overheard her mum on the phone, talking to her friend, whose husband was, apparently, beating her up. "I wanted to grab the phone out of her hand and tell her friend to move out – that's what I would do," she stated.

"Me too! Just leave the bastard and move up North or something," I said.

'Just leave the bastard'. The first time Luke hit me, it was actually my fault. I had stayed over at his, and I woke up in the night, dying for the loo. It was still dark, and Luke was fast asleep. I didn't look to see what time it was. And then I was washing my hands, but the tap in the bathroom was spirting, and some of the drops of water hit my dry, dirty hands and splashed back onto the tiles behind the taps, so I washed the tiles, then the soap, then my hands and the tap, and got stuck in my OCD cycle. And then Luke was banging on the door. At first, I said, "I won't be a minute," but the resultant pressure made it worse, and so began another cycle. After a while – I have no concept of time when I'm in this mindset – I was dimly aware that he was banging on the door and shouting – he had to get in the shower because he was working that day – but I couldn't stop. I must have been doing this for hours, literally. Panic set in, and I was crying. Then he kicked the door in. He grabbed me by the arm and spun me round. His eyes were black. He punched me in the stomach, and I fell to the floor, gasping for breath, but he grabbed my hair and pulled me to my feet, pulling me out of the bathroom, and let go, so I dropped onto the bare floorboards. While I lay there, crumpled, crying, breathless, shocked, he went for a wee and then got in the shower.

Like I said, that was fine, and it was my fault. He didn't know about my OCD then – of course, I had to tell him after that – and the last thing I want to do is drag him down. I'll never find another person who could love me as I am. And, if I'm honest, I need to be in another relationship after Heath, so that everyone thinks I'm okay. And it is nice. Everyone likes Luke, and I feel proud to be his girlfriend, and there are all the friends I've made because of him, and the lock-ins and the parties. I'd go mad if I had to be at home with Mum and Dad all the time. And anyway, where would I go? I need to be here because Heath will look for me here. Also, I earn less than four pounds an hour – I can't afford a flat of my own.

I sometimes spend hours mentally apologising to all the people I wrote off when everything seemed black and white. I also apologise to Luke (mentally, obviously) because I'm using him. But I don't know what else to do. Survival of the fittest. I'm not a bad person, am I?

My dreams are usually vivid, but the one I had last night was especially so. In it, I was hammering away at the keyboard of my portable word processor with my two index fingers. I'd been given the word processor as a present from Mum and Dad – the intention being that I would take it to and use it for my work at university. Except I wasn't at university – I was in an immense abandoned factory. There were great sheets of Perspex propped up against massive, metal shelving racks. There were wooden worktables piled with pieces of wood and rolls of tape. There were clear plastic bags spilling from ripped-open boxes, and everything was covered in a thick layer of dust. It reminded me of Miss

Haversham's room – and I was Miss Haversham, ready, with a full heart, going nowhere. There were no windows, but all the electric striplights were on. Suddenly, I was transported to a time in the not-too-distant future, like Ebenezer Scrooge and his fourth ghost of Christmas, and I could see everyone I'd ever met, in a sumptuously decorated room, drinking from champagne flutes. I called out to them to ask what they were celebrating, but they couldn't hear or see me. Then I realised: they'd all published their novels. My heart dropped like a stone for a moment, and then the panic set in. I was yelling, "But I haven't finished mine yet! I haven't had time!" I beat my fists redundantly at an invisible wall. There was no time. Everyone who didn't care about writing had written a novel, but I, who had always wanted to be a writer, hadn't. "But it's all I ever wanted!" I screamed; to everyone, to no-one.

Maybe it's Karma for my using Luke that he treats me this way. Maybe I deserve it. I think he sees how black my soul is. And he's right, I am weak. I should be able to function without a million drugs and a medical team. I am mentally weak, acting on these ridiculous compulsions, allowing myself to wallow in my darkness. Ironically, I feel safe there. If I'm honest with myself, all I want is to be ill enough for them to put me on a heavy sedative and lock me away so I won't have to be responsible for anything, so that I won't be out there to make mistakes. Won't be out there to hurt. Won't be out there to succeed. Won't be out there to have to face the fact Heath isn't coming back.

Richard

Kayleigh's taken over doing the night feeds. I can't say I miss doing it. I've been bloody knackered these past few months, but that doesn't stop me wondering why she's so determined to get up for Liam now. I reckon it's a hormone thing, or that she's going into manic mode. Then again, something could have happened. No, I'm going to give her the benefit of the doubt and say it's hormonal – she seems okay otherwise. Maybe she feels guilty. After all, I am raising some other wanker's kid here.

I'm at work, and we're short-staffed. It'll be Christmas in a minute, and everyone's called in sick, supposedly with the flu. I don't believe any of them for a second. I bet they were all out at some party last night and are feeling rough now. Anyway, all it means is that I'm having to fill the wrapping paper bins that our wonderful manager, Mr Wyman, has decided to dot about at the end of almost every fucking aisle. Fuck knows how much we've sold. People are like bloody vultures, at Christmas time. And the rolls are all dirty. I've got dusty grime all over my palms. And I found myself singing "Oh the weather outside is frightful" or whatever it's called. If I've heard one, I've heard hundreds of customers commenting that "It's nice they're playing Christmas music, isn't it?" That's all well and good if you're in here for ten minutes or half an hour doing your shopping, but when you're in here for twelve hours at a stretch, it's bloody maddening.

Today has been especially irritating. I was filling up the end-of-aisle cheese display earlier, and the Band Aid song was playing, and I thought how ironic it was that at least half of these fancy cheese packs will be thrown away uneaten and end up in landfill. It's all bollocks. You may as well look after number one I reckon.

And then that bloody tattooed idiot who lives in the flat below Kayleigh came along and picked up one of the boxes I'd just stacked, ruining the display. I don't think he recognised me, so I glared at him until his brain kicked in. He asked if I was spending Christmas Day with my family. Bastard! He knows my mum's dead and my dad is fuck-knows-who from fuck-knows-where.

"Depends on what you mean by 'family'," I said, straightening up, standing strong. Attack is the best form of defence, or whatever. Anyway, it worked, and Will – that's the wanker's name – actually took a step back and bumped into someone's trolley.

"Oh. Well. I don't know what your relationship with Kayleigh is, but I thought I ought to let you know that I've asked her, and Liam, obviously, if they'd like to spend the day with me." Will trailed off. Whatever courage he had possessed was gone. But he had me there. I hadn't given Christmas much thought, but now it occurred to me that everything could ride on that day; it could all be over that quickly. So I played it cool.

"Well thank-you for letting me know," is all I said, and I turned back to the cheeses without giving him a second look.

I kept stacking until the roll cage was empty, so that I knew he'd be long gone before I looked up. Did he really think he had a chance with Kayleigh? I laughed under my breath. He sat in his pants all day painting fruit, or whatever he did, while I was dealing with all this Christmas crap, and there was another delivery coming in while we're still trying to sort this one out with four grocery assistants off on the sick. Will calls himself an 'artist'. 'Layabout' more like. I can tell by his hands that he's never done a hard day's graft in his life. Even so, he and Kayleigh have been friends for a long time. I'm not even going to risk delaying. I'm going to move in on Kayleigh, literally.

Kayleigh

Rich has a key. He said he'd look after Liam while I had my hair cut, which was nice of him, and when he asked if he could take my keys because Liam had left his cuddly T-Rex at home, (I could have sworn I put it in his bag, though) I didn't think anything of it. In fact, he's done so much for me, it would have been rude not to. I had red highlights put in my hair for a Christmassy change, and it took bloody ages. I couldn't wait to be out of there in the end – and on my return – I thought to an empty house, where I could relax and read for a bit – I was surprised, no, shocked, to find Rich lying on the sofa with a can of Krony in his hand, while Liam played on his mat in the middle of the room, happily reaching for his hanging jungle animals.

All I could say was, "Oh."

"Heeey! Kayleigh! Kayleigh with the beautiful hair!" Rich slurred, heaving himself up off the sofa, can in hand. He lurched over to me and gave me a bear hug, before planting a gross, sloppy kiss on my mouth. Instinctively, I stepped backwards. He held his hands out wide, as if welcoming me into my own home, and announced "I'm celebrating, and you should be too!"

"I can see you've been celebrating," I said, trying not to snap at him. I went over to Liam, who smiled at me, and I relaxed a bit. Picking Liam up, I twisted round and sat cross-legged opposite Rich, who was pulling a fresh can of Kronenbourg from the plastic rings that held what remained of a six pack. He passed me the can before plonking himself back down on the sofa. Not wanting to risk spoiling his mood, I forced a smile, took the can, and cracked it open behind Liam's back while I held him. Then I realised that I couldn't drink while Liam was pawing for the can, so I put him back down on his mat, and he went back to reaching for his lion. I felt really lucky that I had such a content little boy. I was also pleased with my new hair. It always looked so sleek and shiny when I came out of the hairdressers, and it was a shame I couldn't do a good enough job at home with henna.

"So, what are we celebrating?" I asked, thinking 'Promotion? Lottery win?'

"Say 'Hello' to your new flatmate!" he said, standing up and stretching out his arms again.

"What?" I laughed, almost dropping my can. Then I noticed the boxes. I felt the colour run out of my face.

"Oh, don't look too thrilled, will you?" There was a hard edge to his sarcasm which scared me. I had to play this right.

"Sorry, Rich. You just took me by surprise!" I said, smiling. "It makes sense," I continued. "You're here most of the time anyway –"

"And I'm pretty much Liam's dad, too, aren't I?" He didn't even try to keep the heaviness out of the 'aren't I'. Could he tell how scared I was? And how drunk was he, really?

The pause was too long. "Umm, yes, I suppose you are," I gabbled, realising that, yes, he probably was. My head was reeling. I knew it wasn't a good idea, but I honestly couldn't think of anything else to do, so I said, "Right! Let's celebrate! I need to catch up!" The hardness in his smile disappeared, and I downed my lager while Liam wriggled on his mat.

The guilt and fear I felt in the morning were overwhelming, and I cried silently as I pulled on my T-shirt and a pair of pants and tiptoed over to look in Liam's crib. Every movement I made was painful, but I didn't cry out. Liam looked perfectly content, sleeping. I vowed never to get drunk again. A harrowing scene from *Trainspotting* flashed through my mind and I shuddered. But Liam was okay, and I did have a vague recollection of getting up in the night to give him his bottle, but I had been drunk in charge of my baby. Again. This shit with Rich was getting out of hand. It hit me that I was doing what I'd done when I was a teenager, drinking to cope with what I couldn't cope with. And I wasn't coping. The other day, Liam was crying hard, and I'd forgotten to wash his bottles, so I just rinsed one out, filled it back up with milk, and gave it to him. I'd been so worried that I'd asked Lucy from the Perinatal Team if that was okay, and she said to just make sure his nappies were okay, and that he wasn't sick, or had a temperature. She came round the next day. I'd cleaned the flat and done the washing, so everything looked okay, but she saw the state of my hands – I'd never grown out of picking the skin round my nails – and said we ought to have a chat and do an assessment anyway, seeing as she was here. She was happy with me and Liam when she left. I'd promised to get a grip, and she laughed and said I was doing well, and that all new mums struggle from time to time, and we'd meet again in a week. And now here I was, hungover again. I longed to pick Liam up and give him a cuddle, but he looked so peaceful that I didn't want to wake him.

Rich grunted behind me. He was fully clothed, snoring on his back on top of the quilt. I had been naked. In the bathroom, I made myself look in the mirror. I was relieved. With my hair down, I just looked a bit pale and hungover. But when I tied my hair back, my left temple was a black, blue and purple mess. I was scared to go for a wee – down there was throbbing and sometimes stabbing, just standing still. I knew it was going to be agony. How was I supposed to handle this? I could picture the scene as if I was looking at it through a kitchen roll tube – as if I watching it happen while I lay at the bottom of my own grave. Rich and I are on the sofa, kissing. That's happened before on more than a few occasions, and I'm not proud of it. Then he's pulling me so that we're squashed in, lying on the sofa. He's pulling my top up, and I'm letting him. Next he's pulling up handfuls of my long skirt, and suddenly I don't want to do this anymore. I try to push the cloth back down my legs, but Rich is stronger,

77

and he's half lying on me now, so I can't push it down. I think I cry out, but my head's spinning and I'm not sure how to define what is happening. He's fully on top of me now, pinning my legs down with his. My hands are above my head, and he's squeezing them together, easily immobilising them both with one of his. His other hand is halfway down, moving clothes around. His mouth is on mine, so I literally cannot say 'Stop' or 'No', or whatever it is you're supposed to say, so I make desperate noises in my throat and try to thrash around. In the end he loses patience. He is up and sitting on my belly before I can move. He hisses "Shut up, you silly bitch!" and punches me in the side of the head. And then it all goes black.

I had to go. I sat on the loo, bit my lip, and doubled over. I stifled my cry by shoving the hand towel in my mouth. Afterwards, I hobbled back into the bedroom to check on Liam again. He was still asleep. His skin was perfect. He was so perfect, and I was so sad that I thought I was going to scream, so I went into the front room and sat on the sofa. My skirt was on the floor, and I could see that it had been torn. There were cans everywhere, and an ashtray had spilled its contents onto the carpet. Near it was Rich's lighter, and some change that must have fallen out of his jeans when he pulled them down, and sticking out from under the sofa were his keys. My keys. I had to take them off his keyring before he noticed, so he couldn't get back in. I didn't care about me. I just had to protect my son. The keys were heavy, there were a lot of them, some of them for work, I supposed, and he had a really bulky plastic keyring. What the hell was it? A toy? I freed it from the tangle of keys. It was a dinosaur, a pterodactyl. What the fuck? And suddenly that Halloween evening, seven years ago replayed in my head, and I crunched up on the floor and sobbed.

Catherine's Novel

All I want to do is run away. My head is getting worse, and all the alcohol in the world isn't enough. My psychiatrist, Dr Whittle, thinks I have – and I quote – "a significant alcohol addiction". I asked him for something that would switch my head off. I asked him for a full-frontal lobotomy. I was crying hard, begging, really, and I would have got down on my knees, but he stopped me by putting his hand firmly on my arm, pushing his glasses onto his forehead and looking me straight in the face, and just saying, "Kate". It was the touch that made me catch myself.

Dr Whittle was tall and slim, with round John Lennon glasses, and thick dark hair. He always wore smart trousers and brogues, and a checked shirt under a woolly jumper. He hid himself, and projected his eminent-psychiatrist persona, by looking down his glasses rather than through them, and by continually scribbling on his notepad. His pen cost more than my car. The chairs in his room were low and padded, and he crossed his long legs to make it clear there was a barrier between us; the sane and the hysterical. I thought of all the people years ago in the lunatic asylums. I hadn't actually been sectioned yet, but I could feel a crisis building. Dr Whittle was the most intelligent person I had ever met, but I still wondered if he had really guessed what horrors lurked in my head. I imagine forensic pathologists to be the same – aloof – seeing the body as a thing rather than a person, to facilitate them to cope with the job they have to do.

So, to have actually touched me, I must have shocked him. I looked down at my hands – they were fists clasping handfuls of hair. I noticed my arms. I had pushed my sleeves back because it was so warm in the little room. My forearms were bruised and bleeding.

"Kate," he repeated. "I've been wanting to ask you a question for a while, and I'm going to ask it now. When you come to see me for these tri-monthly appointments, are you acting? I don't mean to cause offence, but it seems to me that things are a lot worse than you've led me to believe."

I put my head in my hands and sobbed.

"Do you feel safe, Kate?" he asked, quietly.

I realised I was rocking back and forth in my chair, so I stopped and calmed myself. I had to be careful.

"Yes, I'm okay," I said, bringing my head up so that I could look him in the eye. In my peripheral vision I could see his plastic dancing cactus moving on the table nearest to me, by the eternal box of tissues, and suddenly everything was so bizarre that I laughed. Dr Whittle's eyes held a look of concern, but he noticed what I'd seen, and permitted himself a small smile.

In the end I walked out of his office on the top floor of the hospital with a prescription for diazepam, and another card with the details for the Crisis Team on it.

I'd taken a chance. I'd asked Tasha for a day off work as soon as the letter bearing my appointment with Dr Whittle had arrived. Luke had never called in to see me at work, and I knew he was working long shifts again because it was getting near to Christmas. I had to go to my appointment, but I knew Luke would go ballistic if he found out, so having a secret day off was my only option. Plus I had something else I wanted to do.

It was a relief to finally arrive back at the automatic doors of the hospital entrance. The heavy, dull smell of hospital lunches saturated every molecule of air in there. I've never known a smell like it, worse than a pub full of smokers for getting into your clothes and hair. (I noticed two wispy grey hairs at the front of my centre parting yesterday which told me that my life was passing, and I hadn't done anything with it yet. But that was just one more thing on an ever-growing list of worries). Thankfully, I'd calmed down. My head was full of the static noise like when the TV channels used to close down for the night, and your set is still switched on. If I could cultivate this mental state at will, I'd live in it all the time. It was a perfect state to be in to have my Tarot cards read.

I'd noticed the A5 sign in the window of what everyone called 'the hippy shop', when I'd passed there on the way to the Barge with Lola one Saturday evening. She'd been in there loads and had recently applied for a weekend job they'd advertised. She hadn't heard back from them yet. I'd been too scared to go in there on my own. What if I didn't know enough about Wicca, and they thought I was a fraud, or worse – a wannabe? Also, Lola had the look, with her long floaty skirts, and cardigans and scarves. She looked like she'd smell of joss sticks, and in the summer, she did put flowers in her long, tangled hair. I'd tried. I'd got all the skirts and stuff, but all the fabric just got in the way, and hampered my movements, and I could never concentrate with hair in my face. So I just stayed in my jeans and T-shirts and ponytail, but I teamed it with DM boots and lots of bead bracelets.

I'd booked the Tarot session for an hour after my meeting with Dr Whittle, which gave me ample time to walk up there, go to the loo and get a can of Diet Pepsi, and read for a bit in the public garden where the bus station used to be – the one with the monument dedicated to all the soldiers who fought in the war (I never knew which one) in Burma. I was rereading the well-thumbed book on Wicca that Lola had given to me. She'd bought it when she'd bunked off and gone to Glastonbury one day. She'd spent most of the day, she said, in the bookshop. I'd been skimming through the book, looking for love spells, or truth spells – something that would help me make sense of Heath's actions, and make things all right between us again. Also, Lola and I would be doing our winter solstice blessing again soon and I wanted to be able to say it off by heart this year. And while I was sitting there, on the bench in the corner, looking over the rose garden towards the multi-storey car park, I saw him. It was definitely him. I knew the soft, yellow hair and bouncing walk, and my breath caught in my throat. I whispered "Heath!", and realised I should shout it and run after him, but my book and glasses and can of Diet Pepsi were on the bench, and what if someone nicked them? So I gathered them together as quickly as I could, spilling some Pepsi on my beloved book, shoving everything into my rucksack. I stumbled and ran out of the park, via the meandering paths, not through the roses, and headed down the hill, shouting "Heath!" I stopped running suddenly and scanned the heads of the people around me. I panicked, desperately searching. An old couple turned towards me, presumably to see why I was shouting, and I mouthed 'Sorry' at them before running on, because I could see Heath disappearing into the multi-storey.

I ran on down, my rucksack bumping on my back, the strap cutting into my hand, which held it on my left shoulder. Most of the Pepsi had slopped out of the can, so I chucked it into a bin on the way. Things, getting in the way all the time.

The weak winter sun had never got round to warming the pedestrian entrance to the car park. It was cold and dark when I stepped under the arch and let my eyes grow accustomed to the gloom. I couldn't see Heath. No-one was there, and on this middle level there were only a few cars. I started looking for Heath's car, but it occurred to me that the last time I'd seen him, he'd said that it had failed its MOT, so he might have got a new one by now. I had no option but to look in all the cars on all the levels. I worked methodically, starting at the top. How could there possibly be no-one around? Surely somebody would have finished their shopping by now. I hadn't heard a car start up, either, so he must be in here somewhere. I felt like a hunter, and it did cross my mind that my behaviour was stalker-esque, but what else could I do?

Maybe he hadn't heard me shout. Maybe it hadn't been him who'd come in here. My overwhelming feeling, though, was 'He's hiding from me'. Again. My head became familiarly hot and full, and I automatically started to rub my forehead, hard. It had become habitual. I wished again for a full-frontal lobotomy. I stopped my search, dropped my rucksack, and rubbed my forehead again until the outside felt hotter than the inside. I remembered my Tarot card appointment and looked at my watch. If I left now, I could still make it, but that would mean abandoning my search. An involuntary sob escaped my mouth. I was still on the top level of the car park. I picked up my stuff, and leaned on a wall, looking over the edge. I wondered if it was high enough. Then, out of nowhere, I thought of Dr Whittle's dancing cactus. I popped a couple of diazepam instead.

Richard

I remember every second of last night. I shouldn't have let myself get so pissed, but I was celebrating – I'd got into Kayleigh's home, and I would destroy her from the inside out, like the larvae of a wasp. And where I'd recently been duped into thinking she was all right, the ease with which she'd joined me in a drinking session, while there was no-one but us to look after her baby son, was ridiculous, and showed that she really didn't give a shit about him. She deserves this.

I've moved a few boxes of my stuff in, too, just to cement things. It's only clothes and CDs. I don't really have a lot of possessions anyway. I've decided to let her think I've given up my flat. I'm earning enough to do this for a month. It won't take any longer than that. Then the kid's dad will have to come out of the woodwork. From what Kayleigh has told me about her parents, they won't exactly be fighting to take Liam on. Then I'll go after him. But one thing at a time.

I knew Kayleigh was crying. She was standing by the crib, holding Liam, in just her knickers and a T-shirt. I knew she felt bad about having been so pissed last night. Good. She should. The thing was, what did she remember, and how would she react to it? I grunted to make her think I was still asleep. She went into the bathroom for ages, and I must have drifted off again. When I awoke, Kayleigh was standing by Liam's crib again, holding him. After a while, she realised she needed to change, feed, and dress him. She put him back in his basket like he was made out of spun sugar, while she got some wipes, a nappy and some clothes together, and he immediately started to cry. My cue to 'wake up'.

I stretched and grunted again, and then sat up. Kayleigh had Liam's changing mat on the bed as usual, so I met her eyes for a beat, before she immediately dropped them back to Liam.

"Ugh. You look like I feel," I said, and she looked up and gave me a brief, weak smile. She really did look rough. I was suddenly scared. I needed to know how pissed she'd been, what she remembered. In the meantime, I'd play it like we'd just had drunken sex.

"Hello, Trouble," I said to Liam, ruffling his little blond head. Kayleigh paused, but only for a fraction of a second. Nerves, or the remains of the alcohol in her system, were making her hands shake. Eventually she said, "Yeah. Heavy night. I know I've said it before, but I really am never drinking again." To make it lighter, she added, "cup of tea?"

"That'd be nice," I said, allowing myself to feel relieved. "And then I'll sort my stuff out. I think there's enough space left in your wardrobe."

Kayleigh

I'd been pissed, that night with Cath, when we were thirteen, and I'd flirted with and shagged so many blokes by that time, that they were blurring into one, but I'd only met one man who had a dinosaur keyring. I kept playing my new-old memory over and over in my head, because it couldn't have been real, it couldn't have. But it was real, and I knew it with a certainty I'd never felt before.

I was on the pavement pushing and pulling the pram back and forth to keep Liam quiet. It was after two in the afternoon on a rainy Wednesday, and things couldn't get much worse. It was the first time I'd been to the cemetery to see Cath since the funeral. I was absolutely riddled with guilt. How had this even happened? The Three-Fold-Law, I suppose. I'd slept with my best friend's almost-fiancé before she was cold in her grave, and he, well he ... I could hardly bear to think about it. Weeks had passed now, and I'd washed my clothes and showered, and the bruises had nearly faded away. The memory hadn't faded though, and what was worse was I'd slept with him since. And anyway, who on earth would believe me? I'd known Rich for years; he was my best friend's boyfriend. He'd been there for me every day since Liam arrived in the world. He was my flatmate. He was well-liked by everyone in this town, and probably by everyone who'd ever met him; he worked hard at his job; he was, to all intents and purposes, a father to Liam, who was now out for the count. Like I had been after Rich hit me. And I'd realised it wasn't the first time a man had hit me – I had been hit and knocked out when I was running away in the park, in the dark, when I was thirteen. I knew, now, that it had been true. I had been pissed, really pissed, and Cath hadn't said

86

anything, and I'd thought it couldn't have been real, and I'd let myself forget about it, and had got drunk all the time to keep it down, but it had happened, and Cath had been attacked, probably raped – no, she'd been raped, I knew it, even though it had been so dark, and I could hear his voice – "Drink the fucking wine!" And it was clear. It had happened, and I knew it. I knew the expression on the man's face as he'd punched me, because I had seen it - because it had been the expression on Rich's face before he punched me – before he'd knocked me out and raped me –

I let go of the pram's handle, and crouched down beside Cath's headstone, holding on to the top of it for balance.

"I'm so sorry, Cath," I wept. "Please don't hate me. I don't know how this shit keeps happening to me, but we always said that if it was love, you had to follow it, no matter what." I dissolved into tears. I'd found a little vase with a forget-me-not pattern on it, in a charity shop, and I put it just in front of the headstone, where I imagined what remained of her forehead would be. Where her third eye would have been.

I told her all about Liam, how he could hold things now, and smile, and giggle. I told her how he splashed around in his bath, how sometimes I felt like my heart was going to burst. I had so much love for him.

Suddenly I had the sense that someone was watching me. Fear flooded my body again, and I straightened up and put both hands on Liam's pram. I felt a hand on my shoulder and froze.

"Kayleigh, don't worry. It's me." Will. Thank the Goddess.

"Will," I said, and as relief washed away the fear, I threw my arms around his neck and cried into his shoulder. He was stiff as a board at first, but I felt him relax, and he put his arms around me, and gently rested his head against mine.

I could have stayed like that for hours, but his hands tapped my back twice, and he pulled out of the embrace.

His hair was blue today, and he looked severe. His manner matched. He didn't prevaricate. "Kayleigh, what's going on with you? Seriously. My ceiling's not lead-lined you know. And all our recycling goes out together. I've known you for years, and this isn't you. You've got a little boy now for Christ's sake. You can't mess around."

As if on cue, Liam gurgled. He turned his head from side to side, and then drifted back into sleep. I started crying again, this time from shame.

"I don't know how all this happened, Will," I blubbed, and cringed at the whine in my voice. What a cop out. "What am I going to do?"

Will searched my face for a moment before giving a small smile.

"I was going to suggest that we talk about it over a pint, but a cup of tea at mine's probably better. And you can pop upstairs if Liam needs anything. He's at work today, isn't he – Rich?"

"Yeah, they're still flat out because about twelve billion people are off sick."

"Great," said Will. He nodded to Cath and headed out of the cemetery. I smiled, but what was I going to tell him? And then I remembered. There was someone who didn't like Rich, and that was Will. He'd believe me.

Catherine's Novel

I didn't feel much different when I left the car park. I thought the whole point of being prescribed diazepam was that it had an immediate effect. Still, I felt like I was holding a secret as I walked back up the hill, and that made me feel special. I glanced into the park as I passed it, and was surprised to see Lola sitting in exactly the same place as I had been earlier. She looked a bit sketchy and was smoking a cigarette. I thought about sneaking past, but she might have already seen me.

"Lola!" I called and waved. She jumped a bit, and then rushed over to me.

"Hi," she said, hugging me. "Sorry, I was miles away. I've got a job interview in Tescos in a minute and I'm well nervous." She cut herself off, then asked, "Kate, are you okay? You look a bit weird."

"Yeah, I'm fine," I lied. "I'm just a bit tired." I gave a thin smile. It was the first time I'd ever lied to Lola, but it felt good. This was my secret.

"Oh, okay. As long as you're all right. Look, I'm really sorry, but I'm going to have to rush or I'll be late. Phone me later, okay?"

"Okay. Good luck!" I called after her, and she turned and grinned, her long hair and skirts streaming out behind her.

She didn't look like she was going for a job interview.

Drucilla had long black hair and dark eyes framed by tonnes of kohl eyeliner. She wore silver bangles from her wrists to her elbows. I'd expected Lola-style skirts, but she wore black, flared jeans, Reebok Classics and a faded T-shirt from Reading Festival, 1994. I couldn't make up my mind whether I was disappointed, or whether it put me at ease.

She walked me through the shop, and out into a back room which, she told me, had a kitchen and the loos opposite. As soon as I was through the door, she closed it, and my eyes strained to adjust to the low light. The room was rectangular and was dominated by a massive mahogany dining table. On top of this was an empty wine bottle with a burning stub of a candle stuck in its neck. It reminded me of being in the Cavern. The only other source of light came from a Victorian standard lamp in a corner. The room was painted entirely in indigo and was dotted with silver and white star stencils. It was windowless.

Drucilla gestured for me to sit at the table, in a matching hard-backed chair. I wondered if they'd got it from the Tip, and almost laughed. Drucilla sat at right angles to me, and flicked the hair off her left shoulder, her bangles jingling.

"Okay," she said, brightly. "Let's begin."

Kayleigh

I'd just got back upstairs to my flat after a tense, stretched-out 'lunch' with Will, during which he'd eaten half a bourbon biscuit, and I'd eaten nothing at all. I'd spent most of the time crying because I was so ashamed of myself. I told Will pretty much everything. I said we'd been drunk and had sex, but not about ... The bruise had gone down a bit, but I'd kept my hair down, and in Will's flat, I'd let it fall further over my face. He'd just sat and listened, and reached out to touch my arm once, and tried to entertain Liam when he grizzled and I was crying too hard to soothe him.

I hadn't had time to get myself together when the phone rang. I plonked Liam down on his playmat in the front room and went back out into the hall and answered the phone.

"Hi, Kayleigh. It's Debs, Cathy's Mum."

"Debs! Hi! Of course, I know it's you! How are you?"

"Well, I'm a bit –" I could hear a wobble in her voice. She gave a funny sort of gasp and continued. "I know you've got a lot on your plate with little Liam and everything, but we were – Steve and I were – wondering if you could pop over and help us with Cathy's things sometime before Christmas."

"Oh, Debs, I'm so sorry! I'm so sorry I haven't been round. It's been, well, it's been a bit mad since Cath, and then Liam."

"Yes, and now Richard has moved in –" The change in her tone cut me to the core. She continued, "To help you with the baby. We were wondering if you had a bit of free time, if you could pop in and see us. Catherine was your best friend, after all."

I was silent. 'How did she know Rich was living with me?' I wondered, before remembering what kind of a town I lived in. I knew that my silence conveyed guilt, but I couldn't think of anything to say that would make it better. Eventually I said, "Sorry, Debs. I can come round this afternoon if that's good with you."

Cath had felt weird about her house from the day they'd moved in. She always referred to it as "my parents' house" and declared that it "couldn't be any more middle class". It was one of the first on the estate to be built, so its windows were ornate and well-finished, its garden huge, and there was a nice lot of space between it and its neighbours. She had no idea how lucky she was.

Debs and Steve lived on the other side of town from my flat – a half-hour walk away. With Liam it would probably take even longer. Will offered to give me a lift. I'm not allowed to drive because I'm bipolar, so I was used to either walking or getting taxis everywhere. But Will said he thought I could do with the moral support. I also think he wanted to make sure I didn't chicken out and wanted to watch me walk through their front door. He said that I should give him a ring when I wanted a lift home. He knew it would be tough, he said, being close to what remained on Earth of Cath, and didn't want me to be alone with my thoughts.

"I want to go home now, Will," I admitted, as we sat outside their house in Will's battered VW. "I feel bad enough as it is, without having to go through all Cath's stuff. I don't know if I can even handle going into her room again." I took a deep breath, opened the rusting door and clambered out of the little car. The passenger footwell was strewn with KFC boxes and Coke cans. Will quickly got out too, pulled the pram out from where he'd wedged it diagonally, half in the boot, half on the backseats, put it on Cath's parents' drive and then just looked at it. On any other day I would have laughed, but I just stepped in front of him and put it back together with shaking hands.

"You'll be fine," he said, and gave me what was supposed to be an encouraging smile, except that he knew that I knew that we were both thinking about Rich.

The doorbell rang, playing *Greensleeves*. Cath had hated that more than anything else about the house. Through the glass in the door I watched the jumpy shadow of Steve approach, and braced myself, hugging Liam even closer to me. The mid-afternoon sky was darkening, and what had been a gentle breeze was biting now.

"Kayleigh," he said as he opened the door. I stepped back in shock. His round, ruddy face was significantly thinner and grey, and there were dark bags under his eyes. His usually neat hair was shaggy and appeared whiter. He seemed ten years older. He looked ill.

"Come in," he urged, kindly. "Your little 'un will be getting cold."

Steve led me into the kitchen where Debs was standing at the sink, staring out of the window into the back garden. The draining board was stacked with steaming plates and mugs, as if she was washing up for the first time in days. Debs' hands were motionless in the water. I stood behind one of the kitchen chairs tucked under the pine table. Steve walked up to his wife and put a hand on her shoulder.

Debs jumped a bit and turned around, pulling her hands out of the soapy water. They were red and steamed like the plates. Uncharacteristically, her nails were unpolished, but it was her face that made me gasp. It was the first time I'd ever, in all the years I'd known her, seen her without make-up. She'd even worn lipstick to Cath's funeral. I hadn't been able to see her eyes then, as she'd hidden them behind big sunglasses. Her usually creamy complexion was dull and grey, and, like her husband's, her cheeks had sunken in. She had the high cheekbones that Cath had inherited, and now they were almost cutting through her skin. Her eyes were so crimson and dark, she could have gone ten rounds in a boxing ring. It was painful to look at.

"Kayleigh," she said, and came over, hugging me as I stood there with Liam in my arms, while Steve lugged Liam's pram into their hall. I felt tears sting behind my eyes, and Debs pulled me tighter. I rested my head against hers and we both cried. Liam started squirming, so I rested him on my hip and rocked him.

"Kayleigh, love, I'm sorry for snapping at you on the phone earlier. It just seems like the world's gone mad." She broke off to wipe her eyes and blow her nose.

"No, I'm sorry, Debs. I was just talking to Will about it earlier. I don't know what's happening. I'm in a situation with Rich, and I don't know how to get out of it. I didn't mean for him to move in. He just kind of ended up there, and he's been so good to me with Liam and that. He stayed with me for the whole birth, and he's done loads of night feeds – and I – I –" I broke off. I was babbling. I didn't know how much to tell them.

"You don't have to explain, love. We know you both loved Cathy. We appreciate that it's difficult for you, too."

Liam was squirming more insistently now. "Debs, would it be okay if I just gave Liam some milk?"

"Of course, love. You go ahead and I'll dry up these dishes," Cath's mum said.

"And I'll make myself scarce!" said Steve, who was already halfway down the hall.

"It's okay, I'm not breastfeeding," I called after him, but he put his hands over his ears and kept walking. I smiled, and reached into my ever-present rucksack to find Liam's bottle. Debs and Steve were more like parents to me than my actual mum and dad. I felt the tears sting again, and kissed Liam's perfect little nose. He smiled his gummy smile, and I sat there at the kitchen table, holding his warm, little body while he sucked.

I was silent and smiling as tears streamed down my face, and I thought about Cath, and the last time I'd seen her face. It had been when I'd seen her in the Chapel of Rest. I hadn't said 'goodbye' to her the day I'd hauled her body out of the vermillion soup she'd died in. Too much had been happening for me to register that would be the last time that I would see her. Also, I needed to return her ring, to make sure she would be buried with it. Then both the Goddess and I would be with her, and she wouldn't lie there in the dark, alone.

The Chapel of Rest was about two minutes' walk from my

flat. I thought it couldn't have possibly been built in a worse place. For a start, it was just a stone's throw from the factory that had been responsible for the permanence and growth of the town. Rows of 'factory houses' lined the narrow streets around the factory itself, which had sprawled in line with technological development. If you worked for Farefield Fabrics, you could get a two-bedroom house with a large garden and central heating for about £150 a month. People sometimes talked about 'living in Farefield' because it was a kind of village of its own down there, with a row of shops that led from the river to the factory. There was a butcher, an offy, and a general grocery store. There was also a bike shop run and owned by a bloke called Keith.

Keith was so thin and lanky, it looked like he'd been stretched on a rack. He'd been racing bikes, fixing bikes, and assembling bikes since he was a child. And although he was thin, he was bloody strong. He had lived next door to the shop all his life and knew everyone in the town. He'd taught most of them to ride. Actually, he'd taught me how to ride. He had known Cath's parents from school. It was him I banged into as I pushed Liam, in his pram, past the Riverboat that day. I said hello. I'd known Keith pretty much my whole life, and although I didn't feel like talking, I couldn't pretend I hadn't seen him.

"Kayleigh-Amanda! All right, kiddo? Long time no see! How are you doing? I was so sorry to hear about Cathy. You two were like twins. Ah, kiddo, I didn't mean to upset you." Keith came up and put a cable-like arm around my shoulder, as I struggled to keep the tears and sobs inside. He smelt of oil and tobacco. "She was lucky to have you as a friend. God knows she needed one, going out with that loser," he mumbled.

He stepped away, pulled a pouch of tobacco out of his jeans, and started to roll a cigarette. I fished in my bag for a cigarette and blew my nose. Then I registered what he had said.

"'Loser'?" I said, "Who, Rich?"

"Oh. Yeah, I never liked him. He's got bad 'un written all

over him," Keith quickly replied.

"What?! Everyone loves him! He's pretty much running Tesco. Everyone down the Riverboat loves him," I countered, but I'd started to question what I was saying before I finished the sentence.

Keith gave a thin smile. "Mmm, is that true? Do you, or any of his fans, know what he did before he came here?"

"Yeah. He used to live in Somerset, I think, and he worked in Finefare. That's how he got the deputy's job at Tesco. He had so much experience!" I was indignant. I found myself standing up for Rich. After all, Cath would have married him, and he had been there for me the day Liam was born. I was confused. And I was on my way to see my best friend for the very last time. I felt my face start to crumble. Keith noticed, and put a hand on my shoulder.

"Look, Kayleigh. You're a lovely girl, and I've known you all your life. You've just lost your best friend, and I'm sorry. But go careful with Richard, kiddo. I'll say no more than this. As someone who knew his family, he's a bit of a Jekyll and Hyde, that's all–"

"Keith! Phone!" A thin, young lad called from the shop doorway.

Keith patted my shoulder and, with a quick smile, jogged back over the road to answer the call.

And then I smiled at the patterns in life and felt under my top for Cath's ring on the long chain round my neck. I was *meant* to see Keith today. I'd got the ring from him – kind of – in the first place. It was years ago, and my parents had taken me to his shop to get a new bike for my birthday. It was one of the few occasions I remember us doing something as a family. The grown-ups had been talking about someone they'd known from school that had died. Why did no-one ever leave here?! I had been wandering around the shop looking at the girls' bikes. I saw a purple one I liked and turned round to the counter to tell Mum and Dad. They were laughing about something, so I went over to look at an upside-down bike that Keith had been working on. There were spanners and things around it, and then something shiny caught my eye. It was the ring. I glanced back at Mum and Dad, but everyone was still talking, so I picked up the ring, and saw that it was a pentagram. It didn't look like anything Keith or any of the shop boys would wear, and anyway, it was tiny. I could hardly get it on myself. I thought that a customer must have lost it. Then I thought Cath would like it. It would cheer her up, and remind her that everything was going to be all right. So I'd hidden it safely in one of my socks, taken it home, and given it to Cath on her birthday.

And now I had seen Keith on the way to see Cath, and it felt like things had come full circle.

Richard

The store manager, Mr Wyman, or Rob to anyone wearing a suit, brought in a Santa hat for me to wear today. I'd avoided all that crap until now, but as it's Christmas Eve Eve (Jesus!), he wants everyone to "put their festive faces on". Apparently "it's nice to do anyway, but if you're all in the spirit, our customers will be, which will prompt them to make more purchases," and hopefully, we'll "smash our targets this year". Which better bloody mean a better bloody bonus. Everyone whooped and cheered. What a bunch of wankers.

We were so busy that lunchtime came and went, and I had to keep relieving (no pun intended) the girls on the checkouts because they weren't even getting time to piss. Then I was stacking, because it seems that the grocery assistants have a rota for being off sick, and everyone in this godforsaken town is planning to live the rest of their miserable lives on mince pies and cheese.

By three o'clock I was well and truly fucked off, so I went up to the office and told Wyman that I was going to pass out if I didn't get a coffee, and I took myself off to the Riverboat for half an hour. On the way down I saw Cath's brother, Tim. I hadn't bumped into him in ages, and when we were about to pass on the pavement, I found a smile from somewhere and said, "All right, mate?"

I wasn't expecting him to kiss me or to give me a bear hug, but I was honestly shocked when he walked angrily past me, and shoved me with his shoulder.

"Oi! What the fuck?!" I turned quickly and grabbed him by the elbow, pulling him round to face me. He forcefully shook his arm free, and gave me a look so dark, I was actually scared for a second.

"Fuck off!" Tim spat. Before he could turn and storm off, I pushed him hard with both hands.

"What the fuck is your problem?" I shouted, squaring myself up.

"You. You are my problem, *brother in law*," he said, his voice dripping with anger and sarcasm.

"Why? If you've got something to say, go and bloody say it!" I said, taking a step towards him. And then, from nowhere, I said, "She slit her fucking wrists!"

Tim bristled. "Don't you *dare* play the heartbroken fucking victim! My *sister* killed herself! Do you have *any* idea how that feels? You knew Cathy, what, about a year, *and* you were virtually engaged. You were about join our *family*, and as soon as she's dead you go and shag her best mate. And then move in with her! Nice! That's really fucking nice."

Ah. So word had got out already. I should have expected that, in a town this size. I needed to calm this right down and gather my thoughts, but all I wanted to do was kick his head in and scream at him about my mother. I put my hands in my pockets and clenched my fists, pushing the urge down. I tried to organise my face into a regretful expression.

"Look, mate, I know it might seem like that, but Kayleigh's the closest person to Cath for me. She needed some help. I happened to be passing when she went into labour – in all honesty, if Cath had still been alive, I'd have still been this involved with her and Liam anyway! And then we had one too many, and it all got out of hand. Come on, mate, I'm on my lunch break, come and have a quick pint and we can sort this out."

The angry shape of Tim's thick, Gallagher-like eyebrows softened a bit, and the tension in my shoulders lessened.

"All right. Look, sorry, mate. Everything's got a bit fucked up, you know?"

I relaxed. I had him. I turned back in the direction of the Riverboat and slapped his meaty shoulder. "I know, mate. I know."

Kayleigh

Blinking back tears for the umpteenth time that day, I took the few short steps to the Chapel of Rest and realised that I was probably late.

I'd never paid any attention to the building before. I'd been fortunate enough never to have had cause to, and realised that I didn't know how to get in. I walked around the building, past the big garage doors – for the hearses, I thought. Or ambulances? It gave me the creeps to think that Cath had entered this building in her own clothes, her face still open to the touch of the sun and the wind, and that she would leave it, covered up forever. My eyes stung again, and I walked around a windowless gable before arriving at an ordinary PVC door, with an ordinary doorbell, flanked by two little windows hung with thick net curtains, like your grandma would have. It looked so much like a normal front door that I went around again. Finding no other option when I got back to the door, I pressed the doorbell. I wondered, fleetingly, if it would play *Greensleeves*, but as soon as my arm had fallen back down to my side, a sombre, well-dressed man in his late thirties opened the door, and stepped to the side to allow me to enter.

Weirdly (but what was I expecting?), the inside of the Chapel of Rest looked like a 1970s council house. The man ushered me into a front room that was empty except for a few hard-backed chairs lined up against the wall, and broke his silence to say, "Hello, Kayleigh. Please have a seat while I get Catherine ready for you." The curtains were red velvet, and the carpet was thick. Once he'd closed the door behind him, it was completely still and silent – muted – like when you open your front door in the morning to find that it has been snowing heavily all night. Liam was sleeping fitfully, and though I was trying to gather my thoughts and psych myself up for seeing Cath actually, really dead, I kept sending up prayers that Liam would sleep through this, and sang the theme tune to *Button Moon* under my breath. On top of all this, I wondered what the man had meant when he said he was going to 'get' Cath 'ready'. Then I registered that there was no clock in this room, and that, in spite of all the soft furnishings, it was quite cold.

He was gone for what seemed like only a few minutes, and when he returned, he looked pointedly at Liam's pram, and said, "Are you sure you want to do this?" But I was already nodding before he had finished the sentence.

"I'll be at the top of the stairs," the man said. "Whenever you're ready." I nodded again and pushed Liam's pram through the door opposite the quiet room, while the man held it open. I looked back at him for reassurance and he said, "I'll be right there." He nodded to the staircase. I stepped slowly forward, and he closed the door softly behind me.

The new room was the same size as the other, with the same thick furnishings. Chairs were positioned like the pews in a church, and there was Cath's coffin where the altar would have been. Tall candles stood around it, protectively, reverently. I walked up this mockery of an aisle, pushing my baby, like a bride in some fucked-up wedding. The hood of Liam's pram was still up so, if he woke, he couldn't see anything but my face and the wall behind me. But on thinking this, he opened his eyes and saw the grief on my face. It was too much for him, and he crumpled his own little face up and began to cry. I pushed him back towards the door, smiling and murmuring to him, waited until he had settled, and approached Cath again, alone.

As I got closer, I could see that the coffin was open, and I was hit by the thought that I was going to see my best friend for the last time ever. The clothes she was wearing, she'd rot in. The expression on her face would never change.

I tried to think about how she had looked when I pulled her out of the water, but I couldn't even remember if her eyes

101

had been open or closed. I tried to remember the last time I had seen her alive, but I couldn't. I really couldn't remember. I started to panic. Liam was making pre-crying noises, and instinct made me turn back halfway up the aisle, but I thought about the non-existent clock ticking, and that prompted me to return to Cath. I took a step forward. The inside of the coffin was visible now. Another step and I would be able to see her forehead. Liam was more insistent, but I was at the coffin now, staring at my DMs. I knew that when I lifted my head, I wouldn't be able to unsee what I saw. So I looked.

People always say that when people pass away they look 'peaceful'. Cath did not look peaceful. She looked dead. I knew it was her, but she was different – a Madame Tussaud's waxwork of herself. Liam was crying properly now, but I needed to say everything to Cath. Except she wasn't there. She'd gone and, for a millisecond I was overwhelmed with happiness for her. It was so ridiculous that I started to laugh. Liam was crying. How long had I been in here? I couldn't remember what I'd wanted to say to Cath. I went back to the pram and picked up Liam, and I held him close as I walked back to Cath. I kissed my hand, touched it to her cold dead forehead, and said, "blessed be." Then I kissed a calmer Liam, turned away, laughing, and walked out of the room, closing the door as quickly as the carpet would allow, behind me.

The well-dressed man came down the stairs. "Are you all right?" he said.

I replied, "I forgot my pram."

Catherine's Novel

Maybe it was because I was waiting, monitoring my pulse, my vision, my mood for some diazepam-induced alteration, that nothing was happening. When Drucilla left the room to get a herbal tea for her throat (the sudden drop in temperature had affected everyone, and people were dropping like flies), I swallowed another pill, and then another. Then things got hazy.

Drucilla came back and, smiling kindly, asked if she could get me anything because I looked "a bit tired and 'fluey". I told her I was fine, and she sat back down and produced her oversized Tarot cards from a black velvet pouch. The cards were beautiful, so ornate and thick, with gold edges.

She shuffled them and lay them out, face down, in some weird pattern. She began turning them over, very deliberately, placing them back on the cloth on the table, face up, as carefully as if they had been alive.

She would look at the cards, then look me full in the face, with her big, dark eyes, and talk to me as if I was a child. I was trying really hard to listen to, and understand what she was saying, but everything was slipping away.

I remember Death. Drucilla said that it didn't literally mean that I was going to die, just that something in my life was going to undergo a profound change, leaving me with greater self-awareness. She was smiling a lot, so it must have all been positive. I smiled politely back and nodded.

My concept of time had disappeared. I had no idea how long I'd been in this sleep-inducing room. The sudden realisation of this must have shown on my face, because Drucilla placed her warm hand on my forearm and asked if everything was okay. I put on my habitual 'I'm fine' smile, and said that I had a bit of a headache, and would she mind if I took a couple of painkillers? She replied that of course she wouldn't and left the room again to get me a glass of water. While she was gone, I popped another two pills and took a couple more in front of her, once she'd returned with my water. She smiled a big compassionate smile at me and turned the next card. It was the Tower.

Kayleigh

As soon as I closed the front door of the Chapel of Rest and stepped onto the pavement, it dawned on me that Cath's ring was still on the chain around my neck. I didn't go back. Instead, I strode past the Riverboat and up to the bridge. I stared at the grey water. I knew I should feel distraught, but I had gone numb. The fresh air of the living must have soothed Liam, because he'd calmed down the instant we'd stepped outside. I lay him gently in the pram and waggled his dangly cow toy. His pudgy little hand came up to touch it, and his face broke into a gummy smile. I made a silent promise with myself to wear the ring always. I turned my back on this part of town and walked over the bridge. That was the last time I ever saw my best friend's face.

Feeding my baby at Debs and Steve's kitchen table, with Cath cold and rotting in the ground, it all seemed surreal. I kept thinking that Cath was going to come in from the garden or call down from the landing for me to come up to her room.

Liam had fallen asleep, his mouth still round the bottle. I carefully settled him back into his pram and put another blanket over him. Debs squeezed out the dishcloth. She'd finished clearing up.

"Okay!" she said with a bright, false smile. We made our way up the winding stairs.

Cath's room was exactly as she'd left it. I mean *exactly* as she'd left it. There was a stack of notebooks on her desk, and a pen sitting on top of a pad of Post-Its at an angle, as if she'd just finished scribbling. Everyone always thinks that people with OCD are ridiculously clean and tidy, but Cath wasn't. Her bed was made, but its flowery quilt cover showed she had been sitting on the end of it. The walls were covered with pictures from magazines, photos, quotes and doodles. I heard Debs catch her breath and stifle a sob.

Sometimes, when Cath was drunk, she'd go into this state, saying she wanted to go 'home', but it was clear she didn't mean to her parents' house. After her A levels, when all that stuff with wanting to take a gap year was going on, she'd keep banging on about how she was "close to finding the answers". I didn't know what she meant. I thought we had found the answer. Energy could not be destroyed, rather it flowed from one form to another eternally, and that the Goddess was the Source. I hadn't been in her bedroom for the month or so before she died, because we'd go to Rich's, or to my flat instead as it was more private. All this stuff on her walls shocked me. It was like in police dramas on telly, when you'd see all the detectives sitting around for a briefing in front of a wall covered with photos and papers, in a spider-graph. On Cath's walls, there were arrows connecting bits together, drawn in red marker pen right onto the paint. It looked feverish. It looked mental.

Debs was allowing her tears to fall silently. I looked from her to the walls. It crossed my mind that Cath might want me to continue her work, but then I remembered that this wasn't a TV drama – it was real life. Cath was dead, and this was breaking her mother's heart. I remembered that my camera was still in my bag from when I'd had Liam, in hospital.

"I think we're going to need some chocolate biscuits," I said, softly. Debs nodded and tried to arrange her mouth into a smile. Once I'd heard her footsteps reach the bottom of the stairs, I whipped out my camera and took photos of the walls. I forgot to check if I had enough film, or if I was getting everything in. I just clicked and wound and clicked and wound, trying to get as much recorded as I could.

When Debs reappeared with a plate loaded with bourbons and custard creams, I was just stuffing my camera down into the depths of my bag.

"Right," I said, straightening up. "Let's get this lot off the walls."

I headed for the area of the wall opposite the window that Cath had dedicated to her friends. I'd noticed it when I'd been hurriedly photographing. I'd also noticed that the majority of photos were not happy and smiley. How had she taken them without us noticing? A lot of them had been taken in the Riverboat, and most of them were of Rich, but with expressions on his face that I'd never seen before. Then I thought, shuddering, that, yes, I had seen that expression before. Twice.

Evidently Cath had seen it a lot. It was a look of pure hatred. All I could think of was that last scene in *Dracula*, just before Van Helsing shoves the stake through the vampire's heart (Cath had always been trying to get me to read books she thought I ought to read, but the only one that had interested me was *Dracula*. She'd been right, though, and I love it – even if it does creep me out). Then I remembered something Rich had said, about how Cath would disappear for a while on a night out, supposedly going to the loo, but would return with an often-unwanted round of drinks. She must have been taking the photos. I slipped a few of them into my bag, along with a tatty poster from when just Cath and I had gone out to see a band called Thurman, at the Cavern. It had been a good night except when someone burnt Cath's arm with a cigarette. I wanted to remember when Cath and I were close and used to have fun. From that poster I went on to a section of Cath's own pencil drawings. I ripped them all down and added them to the rapidly growing pile of rubbish in the middle of the room. She'd freely admitted she was a crap artist. To be honest, I was really thinking about the photos Cath had taken of me. Most of them were nice, but in some of them I was chatting with a bloke. One bloke in particular. I tore these photos into pieces and threw them all in the pile.

Richard

"Mate, whatever I say, I'm going to look like the bad guy," I told Tim. I'd got him a pint of Krony, same as me, because I was fucked if I was going to order him a DVRB, which is what him and his twatty mates usually drank. We were sat in the corner of the Riverboat, by the fire. There were only a few others in that part of the bar. Tim shrugged and raised and dropped his Gallagher eyebrows. He took a long drink, and resumed staring at me, so I said, "When your sister died, I didn't know what to do. I was going to ask her to marry me. Everyone knew that. I was deva-fucking-stated. And I guess Kayleigh felt the same. We hung out because we always had, and I suppose because we felt closer to Cath. And then Kayleigh's baby came, and I helped – I would have done anyway, like I said – and then we got drunk, and it just kind of happened. Kayleigh's all right, you know? And I'm lonely, and she needs me and, to be honest, it's the nearest I can get to having Cath back."

Tim hung his head and was twisting his pint round and round on the table. I decided to push it a bit. "Come on, mate. You're a bloke. You must understand how it happened."

Tim sprang out of his chair. "You fucking asshole! How dare you? I'm nothing like you! You – You –"

He clenched his jaw before hitting the table, then took a big swig of Krony and spat it full in my face. I jumped up, ready to kick his head in, then:

"Oi!" Stuart, the new barman, stormed over. "It's Christmas Eve Eve, chaps! End it, or you're both out!"

Tim proved to be as weak as his sister had been. He blushed and dropped back down into his seat, staring daggers at me.

Stuart chucked me a cloth from off the bar so I could wipe my face. I sat back down to do so, then he plonked a shot of something clear in front of us both.

"Things are shit enough as it is with Cathy gone, without you two starting. Drink that, then kiss and make up." Stuart raised an eyebrow at Tim, and I wondered why. Then he stalked off.

Tim and I stared hard at each other, but he seemed a bit shaken and said, "Mmmm. Yeah, okay. Everything's a bit fucked up. We're all hurting. " He shot me a quick, cold smile, downed his shot and stood up. "We're cool, mate, all right? Just don't come round for Christmas, yeah?

Catherine's Novel

I've managed to piece together the rest of the day, from what other people have said. All I've got in my memory is a series of blurred snapshots. I remember the Tower card and Drucilla's expression, firstly when she saw the card, secondly when she saw my face. Apparently I'd managed to communicate that I wasn't well, and Drucilla found my box of pills – all nicely labelled from the pharmacist. I heard the sirens and knew they were for me, but I was sitting on the floor with my head between my knees. There were people rushing about. They'd emptied the shop of customers, and someone in the green uniform of a paramedic was asking if I could hear them. The hand belonging to the voice gave me a white polystyrene cup that was full of black water and had bits floating in it, and I was told to drink. Obediently I tried but stopped because it was cold and "crunchy" (my word). It was charcoal, I later discovered. Then I was in a hospital ward, sitting on the edge of a bed, staring at my feet in my socks. Where had my shoes gone?

And then I got transferred to the severe psychiatric unit. It was a separate building but was still on the main hospital site. Apparently I lay on the bed in my room, in and out of sleep, for two days. All I remember, after the crunchy drink, and my shoeless feet, was sitting at a table in an empty canteen, and being brought some lukewarm tea in a red plastic mug, just like the one I'd had when I was a child. Then Mum, Dad and Tim came in. Mum was in tears, clinging on to Tim's arm. Tim and Dad were pale and tight-lipped, but they looked more concerned than cross. Shortly after they'd sat down Luke came in. His face was like thunder. He met my eyes and shot me a look so dark that a shiver ran down my spine. He said all the right things, of course he did, but his speech was clipped, and he never touched me. Not a hug in greeting or a kiss goodbye.

And that's when it started to get really bad. I couldn't believe that anyone could despise another person as much as he despised me. The depth of hatred in his eyes was intense and unending. I was home within the month. But I didn't feel comfortable with Mum and Dad and Tim. I felt like I had to keep apologising for everything, for not eating all my dinner, for bumping into people in doorways, for being in the loo when somebody else wanted to go, sometimes simply for being present in a room when someone else walked in. I was on the edge now, I knew it. I could visualise the egg-timer sand slipping down whenever I closed my eyes.

The instinct to preserve your own life is so strong. There is a stigma that people who commit suicide are weak, taking the 'easy' way out, but that's just not true. When I was a little girl, I thought that all I had to do was hold my breath until I died, but I found that even when I managed to hold it to the point where I passed out, I automatically resumed breathing. This time when I tried to kill myself, I got really scared after the first two pills, scared of dying (because I don't know what's going to happen – and what if they're right about hell?) and, simultaneously, scared of not doing it right, and ending up blind or paralysed. I was also afraid of how my death would affect my family, and Lola. Please believe me, it was not an 'easy way out'. It was simply the only thing to do.

To escape from the searching looks, and the walking-on-eggshells behaviour of my parents, I spent even more time with Lola. The days that Lola was working, I tried to spend at Luke's, but he kept saying that he was tired and needed to sleep. I should have let it go, but I became like I was with Heath – I felt compelled to see Luke and put things right. 'Put things right' – right for whom? The first time Luke and I spent a night together after I was released from hospital (they hadn't formally sectioned me – I was there as a 'voluntary' in-patient), I found his spare keys while he was in the shower, having just got in from twelve hours at work. It felt like they should be mine by rights, and I kept them hidden in my wash bag, intending to use them when I knew he would be at work, just so I didn't have to be at home. I only plucked up the courage to use them once, and it was like that song at the end of *Jagged Little Pill*, but worse.

I decided, once I'd got into Luke's flat, to go and have a sleep. Sleep was where I could escape. Luke's bed was unmade, which was unusual, so I went about straightening the sheets and putting the pillows back. I saw the earring when I shook out the quilt. It wasn't my earring. It was big and gold and made of cheap metal, from a clothes shop, not a jewellers, and it had a fake turquoise stone. It was gaudy, and it wasn't mine. I was so shocked that I laughed. I went calmly through the rest of Luke's flat. There was a sleeveless, sequinned top in the wardrobe, that wasn't mine. There was a bottle of Body Shop White Musk perfume in the bathroom. I didn't wear perfume. There was a plate of left-over pasta bake by the sink, waiting to be washed up, with two forks in it. I turned away from the mocking plate and made a cup of tea. In the front room I sat on the sofa sipping the tea and blew on it, staring at the wall and windows of the building opposite us, carefully considering how to react. In the end, when the reality that I had been cheated on had fully hit me, I grabbed the earring in my fist and stormed up to the café with the intention of confronting Luke in public. But when I got there he was nowhere to be found. I asked one of his colleagues if Luke was out the back or something but he said that Luke wasn't in that day. He was – I knew he was – but I didn't argue. I imagined Luke, right at that moment, shagging one of the teenaged waitresses in the office. I had nowhere to turn, so I went back to my parents for a bit, intending to ask one of them to give me a lift back into town later on.

And Luke and I spent that night together. I'd been hit by him, and mentally tortured by him before, and I knew that I could still get up and be Kate afterwards. But that night was something else.

Approaching his flat – Mum had given me a lift and dropped me off outside the Barge – he was leaning out of the front room window, smoking. I called up to him. His eyes flicked down to me and registered me. But he kept on smoking his cigarette until he had finished it, as if I wasn't there. I shivered in my T-shirt and called up again. Eventually his head disappeared into the flat, and shortly afterwards I heard his feet thudding down the stairs. I heard the lock click open and the door swung inwards a bit, but Luke was already on his way back up the stairs. With trepidation, I followed his shadow up to the flat.

Richard

I didn't speak to Cath at first – I couldn't. I was so angry that I couldn't put it into words. It frightened her, though, so I was pleased with the effect. I could hear her clomping up the stairs behind me in her perpetual Doc Martens. She slammed the door, like she always did, and it enraged me. Why could she never do anything quietly? I considered waiting for her at the top of the first flight of stairs and shoving her back down them, but I couldn't be sure that they were steep enough for her to break her neck. Besides, I wanted to end her with my bare hands; and I needed her to hear and understand what I had to say, when I succeeded in putting this vitriol into words. I stopped in the middle of the front room and turned to face her. She'd been staring at her feet as usual, and kept walking for a couple of paces after I'd stopped, so she was far too close for comfort when she looked up and met my eyes. Her surprise made me smile. Her evident fear made my smile wider.

"I remember that I once told you about my parents, Catherine. Do you remember that conversation?" I spoke quietly as if I was a teacher reprimanding a pupil. Her face turned a whiter shade of pale, and I saw her swallow before she nodded.

"Oh, you do, do you?" I mocked, "Okay, it's just that I can't believe that having had that conversation, you would go and do what you went and did." My rage was smashing my self-control, and I clenched my fists and my jaw, and watched her while I counted to ten in my head. I had never hated anyone so much, apart from my mother. The feeling, while I counted, was like trying to think of Alanis Morrissette during sex, to keep myself from coming too soon. I needed

114

her to understand what she had done. I needed Cath to suffer. I needed them all to suffer.

"No-one – not the best teachers, not the Pope, not the professors in their universities – knows without a doubt why we are on this planet, how we came to be on this planet, or what happens when we die. They can make educated guesses, and theorise, or have faith. But they can't *know.*" I realised that I was pacing and stopped to spark up a cigarette. Cath was standing still as stone, and I was glad to see her chest rising and falling quickly. She was afraid. And attentive. Habit was urging me to go over to the window and open it while I smoked, but I knew Cath hated the smell and the thought of poison infiltrating her body, so I left the window shut and let the ash fall onto the floorboards.

"Not knowing these things, yet finding ourselves here in this situation, we all wonder what we should do with our lives. This separates us from the animals, but we share their instinct to live, to preserve our lives and, in most cases, to procreate." I was aware that I didn't sound like me – not the one that Cath knew, at any rate. In fact I sounded like Cath in one of her pissed outpourings. Ha! She could get a taste of it for once, thinking that she was above me because she was going to university, thinking she was special because she had thoughts like these, and questioned her existence.

"So going against your instincts – something that some force in you is compelling you to do – is *blasphemy!* And I don't even believe in God! FUCK!"

The control had gone, and my eloquent five minutes was over. I strode over to Cath, grabbed her by the shoulders, and shook her hard so that I could feel her teeth knocking together. I screamed at her. "*She* brought me into the world and LEFT ME! With nothing! With no-one! She took the easy way out! Selfish BITCH! Then you – YOU – with all these people around you, looking after you, giving you opportunities, giving you a stable home, caring for you. YOU feel a bit sad one day because you don't have the answer to life, the Universe and everything, and try to top yourself. You are LOVED, and you threw it all back in our faces. I can't

115

BELIEVE that you managed to hurt me more than I hurt you! FUCK!"

I stopped shaking her and threw her backwards onto the sofa. I spun away so that my back was towards her and sparked up another Marlboro. I'd flung the sash window open before I'd had chance to think about it. I'd said too much, but maybe she hadn't noticed. Every fibre of my being was screaming at me to turn around and check her reaction, but I didn't want to give her the satisfaction of thinking I gave a shit anymore. I'd smoked my cigarette more than halfway down before I wondered if I'd heard her putting on her stupid shoes to stomp off down the stairs and walk out, but then I heard it again. In the smallest voice imaginable she said "I'm sorry". She said it over and over again. She sounded like a child. She sounded like she had when she was thirteen.

Kayleigh

Exhaustion hit me like a tonne of bricks as soon as I closed the front door behind me. I extricated Liam from his pram and, leaving it in the hall – Will never minded – I somehow managed to get the two of us up to our flat. As soon as I stepped inside, I knew Rich wasn't there. The place felt calm, like it had before he'd invaded my life. I could have cried with relief.

Still holding Liam, I filled the kettle with water and switched it on. Even though it was raining I opened the big sash window at the front of the house and felt the breeze move through the flat, cleansing each room.

Then I did something that I hadn't done since Rich's arrival. I lit a joss stick and a candle. I wanted to disinfect the whole building, and to think about Cath, and to devote myself to the growing bundle of smiles in my arms. And to put things right.

Seeing those photos of Rich had been a wake-up call. I had to get him out of my life. He frightened me now, and Cath had known that side of him, too. Then I had a thought that my exhausted brain couldn't ignore. 'Had he treated Cath the way he had started to treat me? Oh my God, had he driven her to end her life? Had he made her do it?'

I went cold all over, and slid my back down the kitchen cupboard I'd been leaning against, jerking Liam as I registered he was slipping out of my arms. 'Had he made her do it?' Where had that come from? Liam started wriggling and gurgling, which brought me back to the moment. I put him in his bouncy chair and gave him his little dangly cow toy to play with – Dad had sent it over from France. I couldn't decide whether doing that was sweet or a slap in the face, but Liam enjoyed waving it around while I finished making my tea, and got him a bottle. I knew it was time to start weaning him, the health visitor had given me a leaflet a while ago and I made a mental note to buy some Weetabix and Farley's Rusks in the morning. I was moving on automatic pilot, racking my brains for instances of Cath looking scared or reluctant to meet him; saying something that I misinterpreted, or laughed off. Why hadn't I picked up on anything? I went cold all over. Had I just ignored it, chosen not to see it, decided nothing could have happened when we were thirteen, that I'd just been drunk and had fallen over and that's how I got the bruise on my head, because Cath never said anything about it, because I didn't know how to deal with it, or, worse, didn't want to? I thought of all the photos on her bedroom wall, and was horrified that I hadn't known about them. What on earth had we been talking about? Were we even friends?

Adrenalin drenched my body like a tsunami, and I almost ran down to Will to get him to change the locks. I didn't want Rich anywhere near me or my son ever again. I *knew* he'd had something to do with Cath's death. And then, like I was in the eye of a storm, I was suddenly calm. I'd carry on as normal. He'd give himself away eventually. I needed proof, or it was his word against mine, and I was on lithium. I was a 'schizo'. I'd always known that Cath wouldn't have killed herself and now I'd prove it. But I'd need help.

Catherine's Novel

I think Luke is insane. He looked like Lola does sometimes, before she has a manic episode. And he lectured me. I know some people think that suicide is a sin, but surely it's an expression of just how bad things are. It should be a time for wake-up calls, not anger, punishment and blame.

I'd mentally prepared myself, as I was walking up the stairs behind him, to be hit, but he just shook me. And it was the look in his eyes, and the way he'd screamed in my face, that made it worse than anything he'd ever done to me before. I thought – no, really, believed – that he was going to kill me. And suddenly I started thinking about Lola.

We'd known we weren't normal, for as long as we'd been self-aware. Sitting in a circle with the other children, for story time, at our first school – we were only five or six at the time – I pictured all the other boys and girls with green lights above their heads, while Lola and I had red ones over ours. We kind of fell in to being friends, like gravity, but what really cemented us as best friends was when they showed us *Watership Down*, the day before we broke up for the Christmas holidays. Everyone jokes now about having been traumatised by watching it as a kid, but for Lola and me it was true. We were distraught. Lola admitted, when she was pissed once, that she still gets nightmares about it sometimes. When the film ended, we spontaneously hugged each other, like we'd just become orphans. And that was it – 'best friends'.

Years later, we must have been in our mid-teens, Lola and I were out at the Cavern Club to see some band or another, pissed as usual. Someone accidentally burnt me with a cigarette. I remember looking at the burn and thinking,

'Actually, I like that.' And later, on the way home, 'Actually, I could do that.' And finally, 'Actually, I'm going to do that because it's the only thing I can do.' I kept my new secret inside, and chatted to Lola on the bus home about music and the blokes we'd seen, and she told me she'd got off with two of them. I hadn't noticed. I walked home from the bus station alone. It was a cold, still evening, and usually I would have been pretty scared. But that night I felt invincible, untouchable. When I got home I went round the side of the house and stood in the darkness, up against the tall, wooden gate that shut off access to the garden. I stank of smoke anyway, because of being in the Cavern, so I knew no-one would notice. My parents always slept with the window open, but their room was at the back of the house, and the prevailing south-westerly wind meant they wouldn't smell anything. So I sparked up my last Marlboro Light (I smoked them because of Heath), took a long drag, and held the cherry over the inside of my left forearm. I could feel the intense heat on my skin. It hurt. Then, I stabbed the cigarette onto my skin, held it for a moment while I stifled a cry, and my eyes watered. I pulled it up and chucked the whole thing down the drain. I went up to my room as quietly as I could and wrote about it in my diary. I can see the words in my handwriting:

I have just stubbed a cigarette out on my arm. I will do it from now on, because it is the only thing that is real.

When I went to brush my teeth and wash my make-up off, I held my arm under the cold tap for a while.

I burnt myself a few times before I decided to start cutting instead. I could cut anywhere, and all I had to do afterwards was slip the razor blade I used, that I'd nicked from Heath's bathroom, back into its new home in my jeans pocket. And one day, when I was leaning against the door of a toilet cubicle in college, wrapping loo roll round my arm to soak up the blood, it came back to me - the Halloween when Lola and I were thirteen. I was watching the blood soak into the toilet roll around my arm, but simultaneously I was lying on the wet grass in the park, in the blackness, trying to turn my head so that my mouth and nose were free from the stubbly, aftershave-drenched neck of the man who was crushing me from above and from inside.

I don't know how long I stood against the toilet door. I think I was in shock. I wondered what that was, and thought that it couldn't possibly have happened, while knowing instinctively that it had. Eventually, reluctantly, I went to see my doctor, because I couldn't turn lights off, or leave the house without checking everything was safe a thousand times. Because I thought that if I didn't say a certain phrase when I saw an aeroplane, that I'd cause it to fall out of the sky, that if I didn't run up and down the stairs thirteen times I'd kill my family. The list went on.

I discovered, to my relief, and often disbelief, that I wasn't special, or powerful, or evil without intention, as I'd thought. I had a mental illness called OCD. Dr Farefield referred me to a psychiatrist called Dr Whittle, and I saw him once a week for a year, two years, before I told him what I'd remembered. He'd smiled sympathetically, and explained that I'd had a 'flashback', and that it was common for people who have experienced trauma to suppress the memory of it. Sometimes they get the memory back, and sometimes it returns years later, as it had done for me, and sometimes they don't get it back at all, he'd said. Although I'd had to relive it almost, I was glad that I'd remembered that night. It was an explanation for my OCD, and I felt a fleeting hope that I could heal. However, I could feel that there was still something missing – and then there was Lola. We'd gone to the park together that night. We'd been there together. She must have known, but she'd never, and I mean NEVER, mentioned it. Why?

With hindsight I recognised she had gone a bit weird, and she'd get really low. We'd been getting into Wicca properly for a while. But when we were fifteen or sixteen, Lola just exploded with it all. Where I was kind of moving away from birdwatching and going down to the stream to look for tadpoles in the spring, Lola's marvelling at nature was increasing exponentially.

She stopped eating meat and her parents went mad. But then they were always going mad, and it wouldn't be long before they left Lola, and went their respective ways. And she did a ritual for every phase of the moon. When we went down town together on Saturday mornings, she'd head straight for the hippy shop. They would lend her books, and teach her about paganism, and Lola couldn't wait until she could drive, so she could go to Glastonbury and Stonehenge whenever she wanted. She grew her hair down to her waist, again to the chagrin of her parents. And she drew pentagrams all over her school folders, pencil cases, and sometimes on her cheeks.

One night she stayed over at my house. We'd gone up to my room at about nine o'clock, but we were still awake and talking in the early hours of the next morning. I was in my single bed, and she lay in her sleeping bag on the floor beside me. We were quite tired now. I was lying on my back, staring at the stars through the gap in the curtains. I'd started thinking weird things, so I knew that I was about to fall asleep. I heard Lola shift in her sleeping bag. She shifted again, restless. Then she whispered:

"Kate. Are you asleep?"

I murmured through the fog that had descended over my mind.

"Kate? Can I tell you something?"

Again, I murmured.

"Kate? I need you to be awake. This is important and I can't tell anyone else."

"Yes. I'm awake, Lola," I hissed. "Now!"

"Kate, I don't pray to God anymore." A pause from both of us. She continued. "I pray to the Goddess. Do you think I'll go to hell?"

This may sound odd but, though none of our parents were what you would call 'practising Christians', Lola and I had been brought up singing hymns and saying prayers in our school assemblies, saying grace before our school meals, and doing nativities at Christmas time. My parents even made me go to Sunday School, but that's what a lot of people did, and

I just accepted that this was how life was. As I grew up I became scared as, to me, God didn't make sense in the world I saw around me. When I first heard the term 'atheist' I felt it was more like what I was, but I was still frightened God could read my thoughts and send me to hell. It was very confusing, and I got quite distressed sometimes.

'Atheist' didn't fit perfectly, either, although I was scared to admit it to myself, because what I felt didn't make sense with what we were taught in science, I still felt that there was a life-force in everything. It got tangled up with what was in my head, too, so I called it 'the Universe'. I saw too many patterns in the world for anything to be coincidental, and the more I learnt about Wicca, the more it seemed to be right. And of course the Deity, if there had to be one, would be female. It was the female of the species that carried and grew new life inside them. Yes, the male element was necessary. Of course it was! But it was the female body that fed, nurtured and protected, and eventually gave birth to new life. The Goddess and her Consort.

However, while Lola gave herself to this belief, I couldn't. Not with my whole heart. I simply didn't believe in a deity in pseudo-human form. Lola embraced Wicca, poring over books in the breaks between lessons at school. She told me she felt "beautiful" when she worshipped the Goddess, and that she stayed up half the night reading and learning rituals by heart, until one or other of her parents would wake as she tiptoed downstairs to get a cup of tea, and would forcibly remove the book from her hands, and turn out the bedside light. One night her mum actually unplugged and took away her lamp and took the lightbulb out of her main light. Lola had been distraught and had stayed up the whole rest of the night reciting spells by heart. She'd looked feverish when I saw her the next day, wide, bright eyes, pale complexion, her naturally wild hair even wilder. She was unable to stop her foot from jiggling in lessons. In fact I could see she was struggling to keep still. Her hands picked at each other, peeling back the skin around her nails until they bled. I was relieved when the bell went for breaktime.

Lola was naturally intense, but I'd never seen her like this. She was so angry with her mum that she couldn't stop telling me. I even said to her, "I know. Lola, you've told me a million times already." She told me she felt "compelled" to study her chosen religion, and she'd been frightened by being thwarted that night. She went on and on until the bell rang and we had to go back inside for English. She wrapped her hands in her unruly hair and pulled some fistfuls out. I was upset to see my best friend like this, but I was also frightened. I tried to cover her hands with my own and to press them to her head to stop her pulling her hair out, but she was stronger, and pushed me away.

"Lola! Lola, you're frightening me! You know what to do on a full moon. You've been doing it for years! It doesn't matter if you forget, not that you would, because it's in your Book of Shadows! Please calm down. I don't know what to do! We've got to go in now!"

We were standing in the playing field by the tall mesh barrier that was erected to stop hockey and cricket balls going over the school fence and into the gardens of the neighbouring properties. Some of the kids had stopped, on their ways off the field and back to lessons, to stare at us. One boy shouted "Witches!" at us, and people started laughing. Noticing this, I hesitated, and Lola took that moment to grab the book she had been reading and open it.

"Lola! Lola, you're crazy!" I was on the verge of tears and looked around wildly for a teacher. Lola was sitting on the grass, hunched over her book, chanting whatever it was she was reading. Her hands were still pulling at her hair. Everyone else had gone in, so I left Lola there on the playing field and ran to the headmaster's office. Everything else is a bit of a blur. I always get that when something important is happening. But Lola's mum picked her up and took her home. Then Lola started seeing the school counsellor.

This turned out to be the start of her first manic episode. I'd experience one of her depressive episodes in a few months' time.

Kayleigh

Shortly after I saw the doctor, an ominous-looking letter appeared on the doormat, and it was addressed to me. I was fifteen – I didn't get post – so my parents automatically knew that something was up. They were still living together at the time – presumably so that the neighbours thought we were a respectable family. My parents hadn't said anything to me, but you didn't have to be Sherlock Holmes to work out that the core of the apple was rotten.

Dad didn't come home till eight o'clock these days, and when he did, neither Mum nor I got more than a grunt of acknowledgement out of him. We would have already eaten by that time, so Dad would spread his papers out over the kitchen table, and spoon down the meal Mum had kept in the oven for him without even looking at it. Then he'd have a shower and go to bed, because his alarm would go off at five the next morning, and he'd be gone by six. He slept in the master bedroom – the room he used to share with Mum. If I cornered her on the landing in the middle of the night, she would always smile and walk into the room where Dad was, but I'd hear her tiptoe out again and into the spare room as soon as she thought I was back in bed. Why Dad got the master bedroom when he did nothing in the house and spent hardly any time in it I don't know. Maybe it was because he paid the bills. The only evidence I ever found in support of my surmise was Mum's red silk dressing gown, rolled up tight, and hidden under a pillow on the immaculately-made spare bed.

I don't know if my parents thought I was stupid and couldn't tell that they hated each other, or if it was easier for them to pretend that nothing out of the ordinary was happening while they waited for their decree absolute to come through the letterbox.

At the time I thought it was all my fault. I was a terrible teenager, with mood swings, and I argued with Dad when he was there, screaming horrible things at him, and I was always making Mum cry. As a child, I stayed round at Cath's as much as possible. I even ran away from home a few times, and everyone from school would be dragged out to look for me. Once I got told off by the local policeman for making everyone worry. And poor Cath. It put her in an awkward position. She was nervy by nature, and I knew it tore her to bits inside, trying to be loyal to me when she wanted to tell the truth, and not waste the policeman's time. She'd pretend she didn't know where I was for as long as she could, but eventually she'd concede. It hurt her, but I didn't stop doing it.

And all the time I believed that I was an awful child who would surely go to hell when really both of my parents were having affairs. Something was really wrong with my best friend, and something was wrong with me. And all the prayers and rituals in the world did nothing to alleviate that belief.

The fact I'd been let down by everyone and everything that, to my mind, was controlling the world, mixed with the deep guilt I felt, and a chasm opened up in my soul. I would wake up crying in the morning, and would cry myself to sleep each night for weeks on end. I struggled to get up for scool, but at least it was a reason to get up. If I refused to go, I'd incur the wrath of my father and teachers. On weekends, though, I'd lie there awake, crying into my pillow silently for hours, pretending to be asleep when my mum came in to check on me. She thought I was a typical, lazy teenager. I can't help but wonder how many people go through life with a serious mental health problem, thinking that's just the way they are, or are too scared of getting sectioned, or discriminated against, to seek treatment.

And then, suddenly, for no apparent reason, I'd feel better. More than better. The world – the drab, grey, hopeless, pointless phenomenon of yesterday – would now be a shining ball of wonder, and it felt as though my heart would burst with all the love I had for it. What's more, I'd be unable to believe that I ever felt differently. Those weeks or months of crying would be unreal to me – as if I was two different people, each denying the other's existence.

I opened the letter that day when I was fifteen and I was High Me. I took it upstairs to my bedroom and ripped it open, my left foot jiggling in anticipation. I saw my diagnosis written down for the first time, written in black on white: Bipolar 1 Disorder (Manic Depression).

Below this was an invitation to attend an appointment that had been made for me, on a school day, in school time. How on earth was I supposed to make that appointment without anyone knowing? I shuddered and started to sweat. And then the anxiety was gone in a heartbeat. There was nothing wrong with me. I was better now. The doctors wanted to stop me being me. They were jealous and I was too intelligent for them. I could see truth and beauty in the world because I was special. I operated on a different plane, and they wanted to sedate me and make me be like them. But I was close to the Goddess and I wanted to be closer to her, to see and to know, and to create like her, and ...

Bang, bang, bang on my bedroom door.

"Kayleigh? There was a letter for you in the post. I put it on the kitchen table, but it isn't there now, so I take it you've got it. Who was writing to you?"

I left the door closed and sat on my bed, my foot still jiggling, sweating again. I couldn't deny its existence.

"Just the doctor, Mum," I called brightly from behind the door. "Cath said maybe we should go on the Pill. So they wrote to me with an appointment."

"The Pill? Aren't you a bit young?" There was a pause. She was wondering if I'd had sex. She shook it off. "Are you having trouble with your monthlies? And why did they write to you? Do you have to go to a special clinic, or something?"

'Brilliant,' I thought, 'I'll take that.' "Yeah. Look, Mum, it's a bit private."

"You're fifteen, Kayleigh, which means you're still a child. Nothing is 'private' until you're an adult. I want to come to the appointment with you and speak to this doctor. What's his name, anyway?"

The phone rang and Mum stomped off to answer it. I smiled, and sent silent thanks to the Goddess.

For the most part, I enjoyed being High Me. I had so much energy, and I could see all the patterns in life. But then, like I said, I'd suddenly be Low Me. I'd seen the school counsellor – the headmaster arranged it after the day Mum came and took me home from school. But I told him it was a waste of time me seeing him anymore because I was fine. He disagreed and had told me to go to the doctor, so I did, just to shut everyone up – hence the letter. I didn't go to that appointment. I didn't go until I kind of had to, a while later.

I'd been feeling down for a few days but had gone to school like a good girl. I tried hard in lessons, and Cath commented that I was quiet. But I just told her I was having a bad day and to leave me alone. I spent breaktimes and lunchtimes in the toilets crying. Cath sometimes followed me and knocked on the door and asked if I was okay. But this really annoyed me. Eventually I told her to fuck off. I heard her sob and the toilet door bang shut. A couple of girls were messing about with the paper towels and called her a moody bitch, and started laughing about her. I still had my head resting on the back of the toilet door. Then one of the girls banged on the door, and said, "Oi! You've been in there for ages – are you doing a shit, or something?" and they all laughed. I told them to fuck off too, and slammed my palms against the door.

That's when I saw the graffiti. Someone had scratched 'Kayleigh is a schizo-WITCH' into the door, with the end of a compass, it looked like. And then I kind of lost it. I had my school bag with me, so I crouched down, got my pencil case, and took out the compass. I thought about what a shit friend I was to Cath, that I'd split up my parents, that I was shit at maths and PE and basically everything, that everyone hated

128

me, that I was useless and a waste of space, and that the world would be better off without me, and that I was going to hell because I worshipped the Goddess, and I rolled up the sleeves of my cardigan and white shirt, and dragged the spike of the compass across my left wrist. It left a little red line, but that was all. It was quiet in the loos now – the girls had gone. I was really crying. I walked out of the cubicle. The girls had left the floor strewn with wet paper towels. I noticed that the paper towel holder was loose, and only just attached to the wall. I screamed and wrenched it off the wall and smashed it into the mirror. Bits of mirror went flying everywhere, and I grabbed a big shard and slashed my wrist before I chickened out. It really hurt. I dropped down cross-legged on the floor, and automatically held my bleeding wrist. I hunched over it and cried and cried. There was a lot of blood, but not as much as I thought there'd be. It was supposed to spurt, I thought. So I was useless at this, too. And suddenly Cath was there, and a teacher was there, and an ambulance man came in. I tried to grab another bit of mirror and have another go, but Cath was holding on to my other arm, and the teacher was kicking the glass out of my reach, and then I was in hospital.

Richard

My Nan, Yvonne, had pictures of Emma – my so-called mother – in a cacophony of frames on all the twee little tables her house was full of. Ugh. I'm no cleaning freak like Cath was, but the bloody dust and clutter used to do my head in. Anyway, Nan had these photos, and I used to spend ages looking at them when I was a little kid. But I don't remember my mother at all in my head. I mean I have no mental picture of her, except that bloody ring. When people talk about her – which, if they're sensible, they'll rarely do – I visualise the photos. I don't even remember her voice, the smell of her perfume, or even if she wore any. For me, literally and metaphorically, she didn't exist.

And it's the same with my so-called father. I have no memory or mental picture of him either. But in his case it's because I didn't want to know him. I don't even know his name. I just think of him as a sperm-donor. And it makes me so *angry* that I was created by two people who couldn't have given any less of a fuck about me. I mean, why have me? Was Emma too gutless to have an abortion? Fuck it, I'll admit it – it cuts me up. Nan did her best, but she hadn't even wanted her own daughter, let alone me. I was her cross to bear.

When Nan died I was the only one who could sort things out. I never even questioned the fact that, obviously, I would be the only one to inherit. I'd decided years ago that if anything happened to her, I'd just empty her house. It was hideous, so I'd just chuck out all her crap, paint the place magnolia, and sell it. I figured it would give me enough money to buy somewhere of my own, far away from here. I did appreciate that I was lucky in that respect – having a home of my own, in my twenties – but then to all intents and purposes, I was an orphan. So I fucking well deserved it.

Nan died, in her fifties, from a stroke. It was all her own fault. She never ate anything that hadn't been fried in lard, and she smoked like the proverbial train. Still, she did bring me up. I'd like to think she did it begrudgingly, out of a sense of duty, but I do actually think she enjoyed bits of it, and I know she loved me. I don't know why that pisses me off, but it does. Anyway, they took her body away, we had the funeral, and then there I was, standing outside the front door with the only set of keys.

Nan's bungalow was on what I used to call 'the old people's estate' – bungalow after identical bungalow with tiny gardens full of gravel, and pansies in pots, circling a massive area of communal grass, like some kind of city wall. This expanse of grass was peppered with little signs declaring that there were to be 'No Ball Games'. Grumpy old bastards! It was torture, as a kid, seeing all that space outside and not being able to play football on it. I used to run about, just dribbling my ball sometimes, but the old git who used to live in the end bungalow used to shout at me over his fence, saying he was going to call the police. So I had to stop. In hindsight I should have called his bluff, but I was a weak little fucker back then. Something happened that changed all that, though.

Nan's place was a two-bedroomed bungalow, so we hadn't had to move as I grew up. I was allowed posters in my room, but she wouldn't let me paint the walls. Having said that, we did a project on dinosaurs at school when I was about nine, and she bought me a dinosaur duvet set. I hated it when she had to wash it, so I'd draw pictures of dinosaurs and stick them to my walls with Blu Tack. I remember sticking dinosaur stickers on everything – even my bike. I really got into it, and Nan took me to the library on Saturdays so I could get out dinosaur books. I learnt all about the different periods and types. I was always bugging Nan to take me to Lyme Regis on holiday, so I could look for fossils, like Mary Anning had. I loved the nearly-unpronounceable names –

131

Triceratops, Stegosaurus, and my favourite, which I later found out was a pterosaur, and not technically a dinosaur, Pterodactyl. 'Archaeopteryx' was a great word, too, but they weren't really dinosaurs either, so it didn't count. But the thing that's stuck with me to this day, is something I found hilarious at the time – coproliteologist. Our whole class thought it was mad that you could study dinosaur poo as an actual job. The whole thing sparked something in me though, and I decided that I wanted to become a 'dinosaur professor' when I was older and told my teacher. She told me that the proper term was 'palaeontologist', and that, if I studied hard and went to university, of course I could achieve it.

I'd virtually skipped home that day, excited about my future. As I got to the door, I shouted "Nan! Nan! I'm going to go to university and be a palee, a palee, a palaeontologist when I'm older!"

Nan had been making an apple pie – she was always making bloody apple pies – and she turned around to face me as I came through the door, her sleeves rolled up to her red elbows, her hands all mucky. I'd come round the back – we hardly ever used the front door – and straight into the kitchen, so she immediately would have seen my expression of elation, and the sunny day outside, and all I wanted her to do was run over, crouch down and hug me, laughing, leaving floury handprints on my school jumper. Romantic twat that I was.

Instead she laughed in my face and turned back to her pie. "Oh Richard, don't be so silly! We've hardly got enough money to buy you a new school jumper when you grow out of that one, let alone enough to send you to university!" And that was that. She wouldn't hear of it again. I'd get a job in Poultry Packers, or the factory, like everyone else around here, and be grateful to have that.

I stopped trying at school – what was the point? I'd had a useless fuck of a mother and a useless fuck of a father and that meant that I was a useless fuck, too. And if *I* couldn't achieve, then I was fucked if anyone else in my class would, either. I played up, throwing bits of paper at the kids on the tables in front of me, pulling the girls' ponytails, shouting out and laughing. One of the boys in my class was brilliant at football, and he'd tried out for Twyford Spartans, so one day when we were having a game at breaktime, I did a two-footed tackle on him and broke his leg.

I could have got away with it, because although everyone shouted and the game stopped, no-one actually thought I'd been intending to hurt him. The teacher on duty pulled me to one side and told me off, but even he was prepared to let it go as an accident if I wrote a letter of apology to Andy. But when the ambulance came, and the paramedics ran up the playground and on to the field with a stretcher and their big bag of stuff, something made me laugh. I was still standing with the teacher who had told me off, and the other kids were crowded round Andy, who lay on the ground where he'd fallen, crying, sometimes yelling. The ambulance men tried to get him on the stretcher, and Andy screamed, and I laughed. It wasn't a nervous little giggle, either – it was a proper big belly laugh. It served him right for being such a flash bastard. I got suspended from school, which I thought was a laugh, because I got to stay at home and lay in and watch telly all day for a month, and when I came back, it gave me great joy to see the other kids were afraid of me. They all treated me with respect, and some of the girls even fancied me because of it. Idiots.

Although I tried to stop pushing myself in lessons, I was interested in the world, and couldn't help absorbing what I was taught, and I left school with pretty good grades, even though I'd tried to not give a fuck about revision. I got a job in the corner shop and had good enough grades to go to college and get some A levels. And now Nan was dead, I dared to dream that I could go to university as a mature student. My eyes watered with excitement as I thought of it.

And then the bitches spat on me again from beyond the grave.

In spite of having planned to simply chuck out Nan's possessions – a couple of car loads down the tip, I estimated – I was fucked if I was going to clean off all her dusty, greasy

133

crockery and ornaments and stuff, and pack it up nicely and take it to Oxfam, but I couldn't stop myself from going through her papers.

I'd been through all her bank statements and that weeks earlier. I'd had to, to notify the gas, water and electricity people, the council, the doctors, the fucking milkman. And I'd also gone through the greasy old plastic address thing that she'd kept by the phone to see if there were any family members or friends who might come out of the woodwork once they knew the old duck had carked it.

There were a few old friends, I presumed, because I'd never heard of them before, except for this one name - Keith. I remembered Nan talking to him on the phone now and then, late at night. Well, when she thought I was asleep, anyway. And I remembered a tall man coming round the house to talk to her, the day I'd been suspended from school. 'Old lover', I'd presumed. 'Gross!' And I hadn't thought of him again until I saw his name there in Nan's childish handwriting.

I flicked through the remaining papers, but slowed down when I came to her shoebox full of photos. There were piles of them, all grouped together with drying-out elastic bands. There were loads of black and whites of people I didn't recognise, presumably her parents, or cousins, or whatever. Then there were little colour ones of her and her girlfriends in the '50s, sat in skirts on gates in fields mainly, or standing side by side, stiffly and politely in front of walls and doors. I cracked a smile at one of her in the '60s, in a tie-dye T-shirt and flares, with her hair all grown-out long. And then one of her in a hospital bed, cradling a baby – my mother, I realised. Nan was looking at the camera, and her eyes were full of wonder and terror. I swallowed back the lump that had formed in my throat.

And so on and so on, until the ones of my mother, in a hospital bed, with a new-born baby in her arms. I was sitting at the dining room table, an ancient thing made of heavy, dark wood, in Nan's north-facing lounge-diner. The carpet was a brown so dark that it was almost black, and the wallpaper was of the same hue, with gold fleur-de-lis embossed on it. The whole scene was oppressive, but I sat there with the battered cardboard boxes full of photos and flicked through. I had my portable CD player with me, and I was listening to Faithless' album, *Reverence*, trying to lose myself in the music, trying to look at these photos without letting them touch me. I was chewing gum hard, and bit the inside of my cheek. My eyes watered, and I swore, and then I let in what I'd been trying to ignore. There had only been one photo of Nan and my mother. Why were there so many of Emma and me? There were too many. I felt like something wasn't right, but I tried to shrug it off, and think no more about it.

I had to go up to the solicitors, Land and Underhill (coincidentally just up the road from the flat I eventually bought and also coincidentally the place where Cath would get a job, shortly after I moved in), as Nan had stored her Will with them. When I arrived I was surprised to find that she had named them as executors and not me. I was spooked. That was a dark place, too and, as I walked up the twisting stairs, I felt a chill up my spine. I wasn't someone who got spooked. What the fuck was the matter with me?

I sat there, on a polished wooden chair, in my suit, looking around the high-ceilinged, wood-panelled room. It smelt of beeswax, and of the old leather-backed books in the glass cabinets. Mr Land was on the other side of his monstrous desk, and he was droning on in a monotone voice. Eventually I stopped looking at his face, and looked over the top of his shiny, bald head into the leaden sky I could see out of the big window behind him. If I had been standing up I would have been able to see the beautiful long garden that ran down to the riverbank. You could see it from the other side of the bridge but, as it was, all I could see were the dreary greys of thick clouds. And I thought, 'I bet it rains on the way home,' and it turned out that Nan had loads of money, and I was still reeling from this when Mr Land read, "All assets to be split between my grandsons, Mr Richard Morrell, and Mr Adam Brooks." It only took me a second to make the connection.

Livid didn't cover it. I stormed back to the bungalow

muttering and clenching and unclenching my fists to stop me from hitting someone, and when I got back inside, I tore open the shoebox, found the photos of Emma in hospital and looked at the babies in the pictures.

Now I knew, I immediately saw that the babies in the photos were different. One had much darker hair and skin than the other, and he was much thinner. I looked at my mother. She was considerably older in the photo with the fairer baby. How had I not seen that before? And she was looking at the camera, smiling. In the photos with the dark-haired baby, she was noticeably thinner, and she was looking down at the baby, her expression hidden.

"BITCHES!" I screamed, and I fell to the kitchen floor and cried.

When I stopped crying, I was calm and clear-headed. I would track down this Adam Brooks, and destroy him.

Kayleigh

The first time I fell pregnant I miscarried. I think about the baby I lost every single day, and I pray to the Goddess for him or her. Until recently I cried about my baby – our baby – every night before I went to sleep. I keep track of how old he or she would have been, and I imagine his or her personality, and what they would look like. I see him or her on the swings, when I'm in the park with Liam, and if there are two swings, and the other's unoccupied and there's no-one about, I push the empty one too.

I don't know why it happened. We'd been to the twelve-week scan and everything was fine. We'd decided not to tell anyone until the twenty-week one, and until we knew that we were out of the danger zone, but we didn't make it out of the danger zone. I'd stopped drinking and smoking as soon as I realised I was pregnant, and I was trying to eat more healthily. *He* had screwed his head back on, and we'd made plans for our future. I'd even psyched myself up to tell Cath. I knew I could lose her over this – I hadn't let things go this far lightly – I knew there'd be a sacrifice.

I just never expected this to be it. One day I was walking down from town, over the bridge, and I felt myself start to bleed. I stopped midway across and stupidly, desperately, tried to hold it in. It was like when I came on my period, but worse. I was frightened, because I knew I was losing the baby. I tried to dismiss the thought from my head, so it wouldn't happen. But I knew. I was supposed to be meeting *him* in the park where no-one would see us, and where the baby had been conceived. And I hobbled the rest of the way, hopelessly holding my belly.

By the time I reached the park gates by the toilets I was

cramping so badly I was barely able to walk. *He* was waiting for me in the bandstand, *his* lips in a massive smile, but then *he* saw me struggling and crying. I was so heartbroken when I saw *his* face over the green railings that I just dropped onto the grass and waited for *him* to run to me. There was no-one else in the park, so it didn't matter we were in the open together, although at that point I wouldn't have cared anyway. It was a murky Tuesday afternoon, about two o'clock, and the air was thick with drizzle. We both knew what was happening, so *he* just held me while I sobbed. *He* was silent, but I felt *his* tears dropping on the back of my neck.

When I felt able to, we walked up to the hospital. There wasn't a phone box anywhere near us, and even if there had been, it would have been pointless to call an ambulance. When we got there, the nurse was very kind, which made me cry again. She said I had had a miscarriage. There was nothing anyone could have done, and there had probably been something wrong with the baby. Then she held my hand and told me that it hadn't been my fault. Then *he* squeezed my other hand, and I knew that we were meant to be.

I still felt this when we were all down the Riverboat, weeks later, all getting paralytic for different reasons. None of us was coping spectacularly well with what we were going through. I still felt it, even when he went home with Cath. I was holding on to a bottle of Hooch, and I followed them out on to the street. I watched them walk over the bridge, Cath's hair blowing wildly in the wind, her arm tight around *his* waist. *He* was smoking, and *he* flicked some ash into the river. I stood there, willing *him* to look back over his shoulder. *He* must have felt it, because *he* did. Neither of us mouthed anything to the other. Sometimes there is so much to say that words become a hindrance. After that night we only had one more encounter, again alcohol-fuelled, again in the park. And nine months later, Liam was born.

When my condition became obvious, I told everyone that I'd shagged some bloke I didn't know at a party, that I didn't need any help, and that I'd bring the child up on my own. I wasn't even sure that *he* knew *he* was the father. We were all drinking so much at that time that it could have been anyone. Except it wasn't. It was someone I loved very much, and *he* was with Cath.

I felt awful about it, of course I did. And I think *he* did too. *He* said he couldn't break up with her, though, because she was unstable. Which was ironic because I was seeing this psychiatrist called Dr Whittle on and off. Not that I'd told anyone. I certainly wasn't going to tell *him* that. But then I didn't really believe there was anything wrong with me. I couldn't work out if it was really love Cath felt for *him*, or whether she was just obsessed. She always got obsessed with things.

One day back along, when we'd been walking down to the Riverboat, she'd asked me what vetiver was. When I'd asked why, she'd looked a bit uncomfortable, and had told me that she was going to make a love brew. I'd let out a little laugh before I could stop myself, but when I'd stopped and looked at her, I could see that she was in earnest. And desperate.

"It's for Adam, isn't it?" I'd said.

"Yes –" Cath had replied. She was about to say more, but she cut herself off. "I need half a cup, and I don't know what it is. Also, can I borrow some of your ambergris oil, too, please? Please, Kayleigh. This is important."

The next day we met up in town, and I gave her an unopened bottle of the oil and an old mug full of grass that I'd picked in the park. I'd cut it up really small, and told her that it was vetiver.

"Oh, you had some!" Cath exclaimed, and put the cup up to her nose to smell it. "It smells like grass," she said, disappointed.

"Vetiver's a type of grass, Cath," I said. "You need to start reading again!"

"I have been! Will it be okay until Monday night?" she asked. "It says to brew it on a Monday or a Friday."

I told her it would be fine and, as it was obvious she had this and nothing else on her mind, she kind of giggled out an apology, and walked quickly off.

I know that was a nasty thing to do to your best friend, but messing around with love spells was asking for trouble, and Cath *was* ill. Adam had said he was a bit afraid of her, and that Cath had turned up at his flat, pissed, one night, and he'd forgotten to lock the door, so she walked in, and he heard her coming up the stairs, and quickly hid in his wardrobe. He said he'd done it on impulse, and felt bad about it when she'd gone, but that she was mental, and had stayed for ages, going through his stuff and tidying up. He said she was muttering to herself the whole time. He said it had repulsed him. That was the actual word he'd used - 'repulsed.'

I've tried to make sense of it for ages, and I think that the reason neither of Cath's boyfriends told her they didn't love her, and finish the relationship, was because they were scared that she'd kill herself. Or them. I pushed down the thought that *he* didn't tell her because *he* was weak, because I loved *him*. And let's face it, I could have told Cath about us, but I chose not to. So if *he* was weak, then so was I. Another thought that I suppressed, was that the reason *he* didn't split up with her was that *he* got a kick out of having us both. There was a darkness in *him*. I couldn't deny it. And that was something that *he* tried to suppress. But no-one's perfect, are they?

Catherine's Novel

I said before that things were never the same between Lola and me after that Halloween when we were thirteen. It should have made us stronger. Instead, we found ourselves papering over a crack. A chasm. All of my relationships are like this – carrying on as if nothing is wrong. Maybe that's just life. Anyway, when we were nineteen, she fell pregnant.

I had always imagined that we'd have kids around the same time to nice blokes who were friends, and that we'd support each other through it, laughing as our bellies grew, holding back each other's hair as we took turns to throw up in the toilets when we were out in town, choosing names, shopping for bits and pieces. As it was, Lola turned up at my parents' house one Friday night not long after I'd got home from work at the solicitors. Mum, who was in the middle of cooking tea, answered the door and told her to go on up, and Lola knocked on my closed bedroom door. Usually she just walked in. She knocked softly, apologetically, so I knew something was wrong. I was pulling my jeans on, a relief after a day in tights and a skirt. I tidied myself up and said defensively, "Yeah?" Lola opened the door slowly and peered round it, as if we were strangers. This was my best friend, and I wasn't thinking of her as a best friend.

"What's up?" I asked, my tone now too light, obviously overcompensating.

I was sitting on my bed with my hands in my lap. Lola sat down next to me on the floral quilt cover. She was clutching a CD case. Her right hand moved, as if she was about to hold my left, and I thought 'I'm going to lose her'. Before I'd had time to think about it, I'd pulled my hand away. Lola let out a long sigh and shifted her hand back to the CD. "I'm pregnant, Kate," she said to the carpet.

This was not how this moment was supposed to go, and we both knew it. She should have burst into my room, grinning. I should have whooped and embraced her. There was a pause.

I wanted to say 'Wow! When are you due?' Instead I said, "Are you going to keep it?"

"Yes," she said. We were both staring at the blue carpet now. The elephant in the room stamped its feet and trumpeted. I took a deep breath.

"Whose is it?" I asked. It sounded cold.

Lola paused and picked at the skin around her fingernails. "Just some bloke I met at a party," she said. "You wouldn't know him."

"But we're always out together! When did you go to a party?"

"It was when you were in hospital. We'd had a lock-in and I was walking back home with Dan, and some of his mates pulled up in a car and said they were going to a party, and I was pissed right up, so we went. It was in a house somewhere up Seven-Crosses Hill, and there was a massive bowl of punch. And I just kept helping myself. And the next thing I know I was in one of the bedrooms on top of this bloke." Lola hadn't looked at me once as she blurted all this out.

"I thought you were on the Pill."

"I keep forgetting to take it," she said in a small voice.

"But you take hundreds of pills every day! You're on lithium, for fuck's sake!" That was too aggressive. I felt like I'd slapped her in the face.

"Fucking hell, Kate! You're supposed to be my best friend!" Lola was standing up now. We both knew our relationship was breaking down, great chunks of rock falling into the sea. But neither of us could stop it.

I panicked and grappled with my thoughts and tried to voice something positive that would save the situation.

"So what are you going to do?" It was all I could think to say.

"I don't know, Kate! Have the baby, survive. What does

142

anyone do? It's life, Kate. Things happen, and you deal with them. We don't all have Mummy and Daddy around to sort things out or to pay for us to get away and go to university! I'll go to the doctor's on Monday, tell Drucilla, at work, go down the job centre and see if I can get benefits or something. People go to baby groups and playgroups. We'll be okay." Lola had gone round to the edge of the bed and propped her elbows on the windowsill, her hands twisting the CD round and round. She was addressing the garden more than me.

"Won't you have to come off your meds?" I asked, stupidly, twisting round to face her.

"I suppose so. I'll ask the doctor on Monday."

"You'll have to stop smoking. And drinking."

"Yes, I know! Thanks for your input, Kate!" Lola really didn't like me right now.

"I'm sorry, Lola! It's come as a bit of a shock. And you know I'm not in a good place right now."

Lola spun round and looked daggers at me. Then she softened, and acknowledged, with a weak smile, that I was crying.

"I know, Kate. Look, things haven't gone right today, so I'm just going to go."

"Lola, I'm sorry –"

"I know. We're cool. Don't worry. I'll see you soon. Oh, and I meant to give this back to you ages ago."

She dropped the 80s compilation CD she'd been holding onto my bed.

"Lola –"

"See you later, okay?" And she walked out, closing the door softly behind her.

Richard

It took me about a week to calm down. I hadn't taken a sick day in my life, but I found myself on the phone to work one morning doing just that.

I was so angry that if my Nan and my mother hadn't already been dead I would have killed them. I couldn't think about anything else, so I would have been useless at work. Also, if anyone had pissed me off in Tesco, I would have knocked them into the middle of next week before I'd even registered what I was doing. It was a funny feeling, knowing that in my present state I was a danger to people. And if I hadn't been so fucking angry, I'd have enjoyed it.

When the red mist had cleared, I focussed on finding this robbing bastard with the yellow hair and making his life a living hell.

Nan had taken me on when my selfish bitch of a mother copped out, so there was a fairly good chance she'd stayed in contact with my – ugh – half-brother, and whoever the fuck was bringing him up. I went through Nan's address book with the intention of inviting everyone in it to the funeral. Nan had actually put some money aside for her service and burial, so at least the old witch had made one decent decision in her life.

Most of the names in the address book belonged to people who were long dead. Some of the numbers were not recognised and others were picked up by people who had never heard of Yvonne. Eventually I was left with one name, the one that had stood out to me when I'd first looked in the book – Keith. No surname, just the Christian name, next to a local number. I smiled. So this was Nan's old flame – or maybe even her lover. My grandfather's name had been

Richard. I remember Nan telling me that Emma had named me after him, probably the silly bitch had been too drugged-up to think of anything else. This in mind, I decided on lover. If Nan had been anything like her daughter, she'd have been having an affair, or just shagging around.

When he answered, Keith said, "Yvonne?" He'd answered on the third ring, like he'd been waiting.

"Sorry, Keith," I said cheerfully, as if I'd known him for years. "It's Richard."

Silence.

"Yvonne's dead, Keith. I thought you'd like to know." I couldn't keep the smile out of my voice.

Eventually, he said, "Richard. Emma's son."

"I'm Richard, yes," I said. I wanted to say that Emma had only been my mother in a technical sense, but that, and any other words I might have wanted to say, stuck in my throat. Why? I pulled myself together. "I thought you'd like to hear the news first-hand. From the *family*."

"Thank you, Richard," he said after a beat. I could almost hear the cogs going round in his head as he tried to work out what was going on.

"Being, as I thought, Yvonne's only surviving relative, I've organised her funeral, and her –" I paused, "affairs."

No word from Keith.

"The funeral is next Wednesday, at 11 o'clock, at St Thomas's. I hope to see you there. You, and Adam." I let Adam's name hang in the air. See, old man? I know I've been double-crossed, and I want to put a face to this robbing bastard's name.

But something in Keith's response tore the smile off my face: "Thank you, Richard. Yvonne was very important to me, and I'd like to pay my respects. And I'm sure Adam would like to say goodbye to his grandmother. It's a time for *family,* as you said."

Kayleigh

I bathed Liam early. He hadn't had much of a sleep during the day, so I knew he was tired. He still fitted in his baby bath when he was sitting up. It was robin's egg blue, with a little boat motif in red and indigo. Liam had always loved his bath, splashing the bubbly water with his hands, and stomping his legs. He loved to play with the set of sea-creature squirters that Cath had bought for what turned out to be him, a few weeks after I told her I was pregnant. There was a green seahorse, and orange fish, a purple penguin and a red starfish. They all had smiling faces. The starfish was Liam's favourite because it was the flattest, so it was the easiest for him to squirt. Bath time was one of the highlights of the day.

Once he was out, dry, and in his sleepsuit, I gave Liam his bottle, then lay him in his cot, and read him a story. Tonight it was *Where the Wild Things Are*. I knew it off by heart, so it didn't matter that his dim night light didn't illuminate the words on the page. When I'd finished, I tucked him in again, snuggled his fluffy T-Rex toy next to him, and kissed him goodnight. I waited in the front room for ten minutes, checked he was asleep, and then went downstairs to Will's.

I knew Will's door would be open – especially to me – but I knocked anyway, out of politeness. I could hear Crowded House playing fairly loudly for him, through his front door. Will was eternally considerate, and never made a lot of noise – in total contrast to Rich – and he was even quieter after seven o'clock, when he knew Liam would be in bed. I imagined Will working in what would have originally been a dining room, the room at the back of the house that looked onto his beautiful cottage garden. I asked him once why he chose that room – the garden faced north and didn't get much sun. He'd replied that looking onto a busy road lined with identical houses didn't inspire him, however nice a day it was. He'd studied horticulture for a time, so he knew which plants would thrive in his garden, and he made it beautiful. The garden was so long that the shadow of the house never reached the far end of it. He'd added that, in any case, he'd installed photographer's lights in his studio.

Having waited a while, I presumed he couldn't have heard me and, thinking of Liam on his own upstairs in my flat, I knocked again, this time more loudly.

The volume of the music decreased, so I knocked for a third time, and I heard his overlong jeans rustling along the carpet as he approached his front door. When he opened it, Will beamed, and I couldn't help but smile back. The purple dye he'd used had made his floppy hair shiny, and I just wanted to touch it. I knew Will liked me. I'd known for ages, but I pretended I didn't because, although I'd thought about it several times over the years, I didn't, in my heart, think of him as anything more than a friend. If I'm entirely honest with myself, when I've been drunk especially, I have taken advantage of the fact I know he'd do anything for me. I pretend to myself I haven't. I'm so full of shit.

"Will, are you busy?" I blurted out to stop my train of thought.

"Kayleigh! Hi! Erm, no, not really. I mean, of course not! I was just…" Will tailed off, still beaming. "Why? What's up?"

"I need to talk to you – seriously. I mean, it's really important. I can't trust anyone else," I said, flushing with embarrassment at my unintentional backhanded compliment. "Sorry, that came out wrong. Look, Liam's asleep upstairs, could you come up for a bit? Please?" Remembering what I needed to talk to him about had made my eyes water again.

"Erm, sure. Of course. Are you okay?" he asked shyly, daring to reach out a hand and touch my shoulder. I realised he thought I was crying.

"Yes, I'm fine," I said, automatically. "I mean, no, no I'm not. Shit, Will. This is bad!"

147

"Okay, I'll just quickly turn everything off and then I'll be up," he said, disappearing back up the long hall. I waited where I was and shivered. It was cold enough in the hall on a summer's day, let alone in the middle of November, but I was also full of dread.

When Will returned, he wore a concerned expression, and stared at me for a moment before he closed the door to his flat. The main door had a Yale and a deadlock on it, but the doors to our individual flats were just Yales. It was only me and Will after all, but now Rich had a key, I was scared for Will. If Rich could murder Cath, he'd have no trouble busting a Yale lock and doing the same to Will, who he'd never liked. Then I silently berated myself for letting my fear and imagination run riot. I shook my head to clear it and smiled at Will and, before I'd realised what I was doing, I had taken his hand, and was leading him upstairs as if he was my lover. Shit! I had to calm down. "Sorry," I murmured, dropping his hand, deliberately avoiding looking him in the face.

Once inside I closed and locked the door, and left a bemused Will in the kitchen while I went to check on Liam. He hadn't stirred.

Will had the kettle on and the cups out with teabags in them by the time I came back.

"Kayleigh, I'm really confused. What's going on?" Will took a couple of steps towards me as he said this, and on reflex, I took a couple of steps back. I could see the pain flash in his eyes.

"It's Richard," I said.

Will looked crestfallen, and opened his mouth to speak, but I cut him off.

"I think he murdered Cath."

Richard

The night before Nan's funeral I hadn't been able to sleep. My throat and mouth were stale and dry from smoking so many Marlboros, and I couldn't face getting up and having another one. I couldn't stomach any more Mad Dog either. The bottle I'd bought from work yesterday had more than half gone, but for all the effect it was having, I might as well have been drinking Coke. I don't even like Mad Dog. I only bought it because it usually did the job. Not this time, though. My brain was working so hard it didn't have room for being drunk. I couldn't concentrate enough to read, or even to watch telly. And music was pissing me off because no-one had written a song about what I was experiencing. The nearest thing I could think of was Faithless' *Insomnia*, but I only had it on tape and couldn't be arsed to fast forward through the album to find it. I felt completely alienated.

I found myself doing something that surprised me – I opened the curtains and lay in bed, staring at the moon. My mother had been a lazy hippy, but she'd got something out of it, wearing that pagan ring all the time. I didn't believe in God, but Nan had, so I'd allowed her the Christian service and burial she'd requested. Mother and daughter had been looking for answers, or solace, or both, and had followed their chosen religions through life. I wondered if, at the point of dying, it had comforted either of them. The moon was full, and every now and then, a large cloud would scud across it. It occurred to me that the dinosaurs must have seen it; a thing pretty much unchanged in millennia. This should have brought me solace. Instead, it made me feel empty, hopeless, futile, and finally, enraged. A cloud pushed in front of the moon; others joined it, and it began to rain. I closed my eyes and listened to the drops spatter against my window, longing for sleep.

When the day eventually dawned, it was thick with fog and drizzle. I awoke tired, but full of adrenalin. I sat in Nan's kitchen in my suit, with the door open, watching the light rain falling on the pot plants and the concrete path. I had the door open because I was chain-smoking. Between puffs, I was necking coffee. Nan had only ever drunk Mellow Birds, so I had to have a lot for it to have any effect. In some forgotten recess of my brain, I must have been sad Nan was gone. She was all right. Well, she'd done the right thing by me, bringing me up so I didn't have to go into care. Thinking this, I realised I was now entirely alone. I gritted my teeth against the onset of self-pity. I didn't have time for that shit.

At ten to eleven, I locked the doors and made my way through the damp greyness to the church. I smoked as I went quickly up to, and along the main road, before turning into St Thomas Street, which led up to the church like a red carpet. The air was so thick and wet that the spire's point was only just visible. The entrance to St Thomas's is on the side of the building, so I walked around, brushing off fat drops of rain that were dripping from the leaves of the big beech tree in the grounds. The hearse was already there. The drive from the funeral parlour couldn't have taken any more than thirty seconds.

I turned my gaze to the right and saw two men in suits talking to the vicar, or whoever it is who does the funerals, just outside the church door. I recognised the lanky old man, Keith, from the photos. Standing next to him was a thin bloke with floppy blond hair who was wearing a blue suit. Blue! To a funeral! The disrespectful twat must be Adam. I stopped in my tracks and, as I did so, the three of them turned and stared at me. Shit! It was that Adam! We all stood there, silently trying to suss each other out like a bunch of street cats. Nobody moved for what seemed like ages, so I shook my head and laughed.

Keith and Adam frowned. The vicar looked from me to them and back again. The church clock struck eleven, cutting through the tension. The vicar was the first to regain his composure and he beckoned us inside.

The old man and my half-brother sat one pew back from the front on the right. So I strode to the very front and sat on the left. Although I stared at the vicar throughout, I didn't hear a word he said. I'd been too angry to prepare a reading, so it was all him, punctuated by *Morning has Broken*, and *Abide with Me*, for which I dutifully stood. Halfway through *Morning has Broken* a girl scampered in, squeezed past Keith, and sat down next to Adam. I only saw the back of her – long black skirt, oversized black cardigan, most of her hair in a tangled ponytail. She put her hand on Adam's shoulder and they gave each other a quick kiss. So Mr Perfect had a girlfriend as well as half of my inheritance. I looked at the coffin and snarled. The fucker's luck was about to run out.

Catherine's Novel

I watched Lola's belly grow, as if it was the bottom half of an egg-timer slowly filling with sand. The day she'd told me she was pregnant was the second 'day of significance' in our friendship that we pretended hadn't happened. And while all her thoughts were on safeguarding the future, mine were on preserving the past. I wrote, but it wasn't enough, so I started to take photos. And when I did, they illuminated something I hadn't noticed before, something that surprised me. There were lots of Lola and Luke together. I'm on so many tablets at the moment that I can't be paranoid, can I? Is he checking her out? I'm down Boots every week taking my film in, wandering around town for an hour while they process it. And when I see what I've captured – well. Also, I think I am invisible. How has no-one noticed me taking these photos? I got a Canon Sure Shot for my birthday so that I could record my time at uni apparently. And because there's no way I can fit it in my jeans pocket, I've started taking a bag out with me. Lola was shocked the first time I came out with it because I'd always said I wouldn't be a girly-girl, and have a vast collection of bottles on my table, wear make-up (that one didn't last very long); or carry a shoulder bag. But now I have to have one or they'll notice. Lola asked me what was in it and I fobbed her off, saying I couldn't fit my lip balm in my purse, and that it didn't feel safe having my key loose in my back pocket. She looked at me funny, but that could have been my paranoia again.

The truth is, I don't feel safe. I don't feel safe in my relationship with my parents, my boyfriend, and now my best friend. I don't feel safe in my home, because they want to send me to uni. I don't feel safe walking home from the pub, or even walking down town in the day. I don't feel safe drunk, but I drink because it's all I can think to do to get away from not feeling safe. Nothing is as it seems. Or, I can't trust that it is. And I don't feel safe in myself. I think I am going mad. I think I need to be locked up.

I think Luke is the father of Lola's baby.

Richard

I got up first and followed Nan's coffin out of the church, sparking up a cigarette as soon as I stepped outside. I watched as the undertakers loaded her into the hearse, and then looked around for the taxi I'd ordered to take me up to the cemetery. I leant on the beech tree away from the others. But I could hear Keith talking.

"That's Adam's older brother," Keith was telling the girl. "Yvonne, Adam's Nan, brought him up. I haven't seen him since he was a kid."

Adam muttered something and then the girl asked a question.

"No way – funeral or not," Keith shot back. "He's a bad 'un. He deserves to be on his own." And he pulled them over to where a taxi from the other firm in town was standing, waiting for them.

I was halfway down another Marlboro before my taxi turned up. "Where the fuck have you been?" I snarled at the driver.

"Sorry, mate," he said. "I had to wait for ages outside the hospital for my last job to get out of the building and into the car."

I jumped in and slammed the door. When we arrived at the cemetery, the driver checked his meter and opened his mouth to tell me how much I owed him, but I cut him off.

"Don't think you're getting paid for this one, *mate,*" I snarled. "I've probably missed seeing my Nan go six feet under." And I slammed the door and ran up the slope to where I could see a few dark figures huddling in the rain.

As it was, they were just lowering Nan in when I jogged up to the hole. The vicar was saying the usual, and the girl was crying, her face buried in Adam's shoulder. What the fuck was she crying for? And when it came to chucking the dust on the coffin, she had her hand in the tin first! And she chucked a load of weeds on too! Then Keith threw some on, muttered something, and led the girl onto the path, presumably so the wonderful Adam could have a moment alone with his Nan.

Adam clumsily snatched a handful of dust, and shuffled up to the hole. As he looked down, I came up close behind him and put my hand on his shoulder. He jumped and nearly fell in. I laughed. The vicar glanced over, but I gave him a smile that said, 'the poor young lad is upset,' and he smiled back at me. I whispered in Adam's ear.

"If you don't give me my money and get the fuck out of town, *bro*," I said, "it won't just be you I'll put in one of these holes. It'll be your darling girlfriend, too." He gasped and turned to face me, saw I was serious, backed away, and ran off towards his bitch and Keith.

"Dad! Wait!" he shouted.

'Dad'?! What the fuck?!

Kayleigh

"Woah, Kayleigh! I've heard how Rich talks to you and treats you, through the ceiling, and you know I've never liked the bloke. But a murderer? Really? And anyway, how can he be? Cath slit her wrists." Will was incredulous. We were sitting cross-legged on the floor, directly opposite each other, and I reached out and took his hand. As soon as I did so, the floodgates opened. I couldn't explain my reasons because I was crying so much that my mouth wasn't working properly. Will got up on his knees, shuffled over, and held me. I soaked his shoulder with my tears. He said "Sssh," and stroked my hair, as if I was a child. Eventually I calmed down, and my gasps became sobs, which turned into sighs. And then we were both quiet, just holding each other. And as I was turning my head in to kiss his neck, Will said, "Kayleigh, have you been taking your meds?"

I could have slapped him. I disentangled myself from his arms and stood up. I thought about walking out, but I'd voiced my revelation now, and I needed Will as an ally, so I went into the kitchen and boiled some water for a nettle and blackberry tea. I got my mug and the teabag out of the cupboard above the kettle, shut the cupboard, and put the bag in my cup. Then, reluctantly, I opened the cupboard again, and got out a mug for Will. I put two spoons of sugar in it along with a heaped spoonful of coffee. Will slunk into the kitchen and leaned up against the fridge. He opened his mouth to speak, but I cut him off.

"I can't believe that you, of all people, said that, Will. That really hurt. 'Once a psycho, always a psycho' is it? I thought you were different. I thought you were my friend."

"Kayleigh."

"Drink your coffee," I ordered, shoving the Ugly Mug mug into his hands. "I need to show you something."

Will blinked his eyes in disbelief at my photos of Cath's bedroom and some of the ones of Rich. But he still wasn't convinced.

"This is bad, Kayleigh. I'll give you that. But only because it's a bit sinister. *We* know Rich isn't the nice guy that everyone thinks he is. But these are just photos of his expressions. They don't incriminate him in any way. And please don't take this the wrong way, but I have to say it, these are pictures of Cath's room. And they say more about her mental state than about anything else. I mean, it looks like she was a bit of a stalker."

I gave him a dark look which almost immediately softened because, of course, he was right. This wasn't the bedroom wall of a happy, well-balanced young lady.

"I know," I said. "But I also know that I'm right. Cath wouldn't have killed herself. She was messed up, and had her problems, but she was sane and sensible. And she was acutely aware of what taking her own life would have done to her family. And to me."

Will sighed and looked at me for a long time. I knew he was conflicted. He was level-headed, but he'd walk five-thousand miles for me. In the end, he said, "Well, if you're sure, we have to find some evidence. You can't just go to the police on a gut feeling. I mean, I presume you want him convicted."

"Of course I do! And I want him away from my son. And out of my flat!"

"Well, we need to do some digging then. Also, it might be worth getting some legal advice. Maybe we could go to Cath's old work. And I think we should tell Debbie and Steve, too." This is what I needed, Will taking the lead and being practical. But – 'We'?

"We?" I asked.

"Yes, of course, 'we'!" replied Will. "I want to help you. You know I'd do anything for you, Kayleigh."

We paused a moment, then I gave him a sideways look and, catching my gaze, he gently punched my shoulder and grinned. But only with his mouth.

When Rich came home I tried to be normal. His face was dark and angry, and I was frightened that I was overcompensating. I wasn't worried about being hit anymore, because that had happened, and I'd survived it. Instead I was frightened that he'd hurt Liam to hurt me.

I'd made some pasta, but my appetite had gone. Liam was still sleeping, so I sat on the sofa in front of the telly, and picked at my food with my fork.

"Just eat it if you're going to eat it!" Rich snapped.

"I'm not feeling well," I said. "Do you want to finish it?" I held the bowl of pasta towards him.

Rich looked at me for a second, and sat down on the arm of the sofa. "Is that all you think I'm good for?" he asked, quietly, cocking his head to one side. "Your left-overs?" He reminded me of the velociraptors in *Jurassic Park* before they eat the fat guy who's trying to steal the dinosaur DNA. It wasn't a helpful image to have in my head and, in combination with my fear, I nearly laughed. Rich noticed.

"Don't fucking laugh at me, you psycho bitch!" Rich shouted and punched the bottom of the bowl so that it jumped out of my hand, pasta flying everywhere. I was shocked into my usual frozen state. Rich went on. "I don't know why I put up with this shit, living with a psycho hippy and your fucking hippy brat!"

I paused for a moment. Rich was draining me. Then I remembered Dr Grosvenor, and a chill ran down my spine. I had two psychic vampires in my life. I had to defend myself. My motherly instincts finally kicked in and I stood up and snapped back at him before I even knew I was doing it. "Why don't you just fuck off then, if you hate us so much?"

I was in his face, and he hadn't expected that. He was flummoxed for a second. "Why don't you just get out of my flat?!" I yelled, and then I did something I'd come to regret. I pushed him, hard, with both hands, in the middle of his chest.

After the shock of my outburst, which had pushed him off the sofa arm and onto the floor, he smiled. He lay there, on the carpet, propped up on is elbows, smiling at me until he laughed.

"Wow," he said, getting to his feet. "Wow. You've really done it now. A collection of photos of me in your bedside table drawer, photos taken without permission, when I was unaware. And now violence against me." He blew out of the side of his mouth and shook his head, still smiling. "You know what? I *will* get out of your flat. I can't live somewhere I don't feel safe, now, can I? And anyway," Rich spat the next bit, "I'm sick of playing daddy to some brat that isn't mine. Oh, and don't worry about getting the locks changed," he said, throwing his set of keys back at me. "I won't be back. But, bitch, watch out. I've got you now." And he pulled his packet of Marlboros out of his back pocket, and stalked out, laughing.

Richard

I made the call from the phone box at the end of the road and played the distressed boyfriend. Dr Erazmus Whittle, Consultant Psychiatrist, was the name at the bottom of the 'private and confidential' letters. The name rang a bell. Had he been the same bloke Cath had been seeing? I'd found letters from him to Kayleigh in the top drawer of her bedside table, along with her meds.

It was the first place I'd looked. Once I'd found that, I'd wondered what other skeletons she had in her closet, and after a quick rifle through her bank statements and other papers, I found the photos of me. I don't know how she managed to take them without my knowledge, sly bitch, but I certainly hadn't been expecting to find anything like that. What I'd actually been trying to do was to find out who Liam's father is. There was nothing in her room. I'd even taken the backs off her framed photos in case she'd stashed something behind one of them. Maybe she wasn't lying when she said it had been a one-nighter. Slag.

Anyway, I went straight back to my flat – Kayleigh didn't know I'd kept it on – and ran up and down the stairs a couple of times before I rushed back down over the bridge to the phone box and made the call. I whispered, too, when the receptionist answered, making out that I was scared, and that I'd just run from Kayleigh. I didn't even have to lie about the last bit! The secretary told me that Dr Whittle was 'unavailable,' but that a Dr Grosvenor had taken on his patients and could help me. I heard the silly cow cover the mouthpiece of the phone and say, "Sasha, we've had another call about Kayleigh-Amanda Tarr, the bipolar with the baby. You know, her neighbour called the other day and said she wasn't taking her medication."

And then a posh twat came on the phone. I told him that Kayleigh had become obsessed with me since having Liam. I told him about the pictures, and about her violent outbursts. I told him I thought she had postnatal depression, or psychosis, or whatever it was, on top of her bipolar disorder. I told him that she'd been hospitalised before. I told him I thought she'd stopped taking her meds. I told him I thought she was a danger to her baby, that I'd caught her holding him in the air and shaking him, while screaming at him to stop crying, that she'd been hysterical, that she struggled to get her baby to breastfeed.

I reiterated that I was frightened for "little Liam," that no-one knew who his father was, that Kayleigh's family had abandoned her, that she had no support but me. I could hear Dr Grosvenor flipping through some papers. He asked if I was Kayleigh's 'nearest relative,' whatever the hell that was. So I said, "Yes."

After I put the phone down, I sauntered back down past Kayleigh's building, over the road, to the church. I sat on the low wall, under the beech tree and, facing back up Thomas Street, I stared at her window while I smoked a Marlboro.

Catherine's Novel

I go through the days living out the inevitable. And it is inevitable. I am on a fairground ride I can't get off. I'd say 'rollercoaster', but there are no highs, and there is no excitement, just fear and despair. I think and rethink every move I make during the days and nights, trying to lessen the damage, trying to pull hope out of the bottom of the box. I live for the weekends, when I can be here, in the Barge, letting the alcopops take the edge off, chatting crap and laughing with Lola. But it's all surface, painting over the cracks, the abyss. I pick the label from my bottle as well as I can with my short nails. Luke keeps on at me to grow them, and I'll be good for a while. Then I'll suddenly find myself biting them again. I look up from the mess I'm making on the table and watch Lola, who's at the bar, getting another round in. She's big now, all over. It's not 'all baby', and because I've known her all her life to be thin, she looks swollen and painful. Her upper arms are gross. But she seems happy, and I know I should be happy for her. She's taking maternity leave from the hippy shop, and she's getting benefits too. Her landlord, Dan, is fine with it all as well. So she's all set up now. She's done it. She's got all I ever wanted - stability, direction, purpose. Her usually mental hair is smooth and shiny, and she's not feeling sick anymore. And she doesn't have to worry about how her stomach looks ever again. I can't believe I feel like this about my best friend.

And it gets worse. I feel like the baby is draining all my energy, bleeding me dry, like it's feeding off me. Sometimes I notice Lola's belly being kicked from the inside. The baby is powerful, growing, and I am slipping away, slowly disappearing, like a morning fog. I let Luke hit me when he feels like it. I used to play dead instinctively. Now I do it because I can't be bothered to fight. I know there is no way out. I tell him I love him in the hopes he will be more gentle with me, but these days his eyes are full of hate. I wonder now if he ever loved me. I have bought a lot of black, long-sleeved tops. And I think about Heath all the time. I wonder when he's coming back for me, because he did love me once, I know he did. I just scared him, that breast feeding all, because I was ill. Because I am ill. I've stopped smoking because I don't want to get cancer. But I still buy Marlboros. I light them, let them burn for a bit, and then stub them out between my bruises and cuts. I am washing my hands so much that my palms are flaking. Everything is filthy and no-one notices. I hate being out in the pub with all this noise and filth, but I live for it. I need a few hours where I can escape from my head. When I recognise that I feel unreal, I can blame the alcohol.

I comprehend that none of these things solve my problems, but they help to pass the time. My life feels like a scene from *Waiting for Godot*.

And there's the next question. Pass the time until what? Until very recently, I'd have said 'until Heath comes back for me'. Now though, there's a section of my brain that questions the sanity of that answer, and I'm trying not to listen to that part of me. And the alcohol and the burns help. They give me a tangible problem to focus on.

Lola returns with my Bacardi Breezer and half a Guinness for her – for the iron, apparently – and starts chatting to me about the names she's thought of for both sexes, that her mum, of all people, is knitting a yellow jumper, so that it can be worn by a boy or a girl, how happy she feels, in spite of the difficulties she knows she's going to face. And I'm nodding and smiling, and I'm sure she can tell that I'm not really listening, until she leans in and squeezes my hand, and says she knows it will be okay, because she's got me. And the tears come so easily. We have a rare hug. She's crying with happiness, relief and fear. She's crying because I'm crying. And I am crying because her baby is growing, and I am slipping away.

163

Richard

When I got home after I'd spoken to Dr Grosvenor, I opened a bottle of Mad Dog – I couldn't stop buying the stuff – and thought about what to do next. I had to get the bitch sectioned. I pulled up the sash window, leaned out, and chain-smoked a couple of Marlboros while I waited for an idea to come.

The next day was my day off. I woke up with a bit of a headache, but I didn't feel too bad. I was in the kitchen in my boxers and socks, filling the kettle with water, when there was a loud bang on my door. "Who the fuck-?" I said to myself and ignored it. I found a cup, put some coffee in it, and then something made me go for a shifty look out of the window. Before I got there, the door banged again. I looked out. It was the pigs. What the fuck?

Not bothering to put anything else on, I stomped down the stairs, shouting, "Hang on!" The pig banged again, which wound me up, and I wrenched the door open, but realised that I needed to be nice, so I forced my mouth into what I hoped looked like a confused smile.

"Mr Morrell?" the pig asked.

"Yes," I said. "What can I do for you, officer?"

"We'd like a word, please, Mr Morrell. Can we come in?"

"Can I ask what this is about?"

"We've had a complaint," he said, smiling. "It's probably a misunderstanding, so perhaps we could come in and sort it out. And perhaps you could put some clothes on for the sake of my female colleague."

I was reeling. I showed the pigs out, shut the door, and leaned against it for a moment. Then I went back upstairs, made a fresh cup of coffee, and slumped on the sofa to think.

They'd refused to tell me who'd made the complaint. Apparently it had been anonymous. but it was pretty fucking obvious. It had to be Will. The ceilings in Kayleigh's flat must be thinner than I thought because "a member of the public" had heard some "disturbance" in Kayleigh's flat "on several occasions", and had called them because he/she was "worried for Kayleigh's safety and for the safety of her baby", and because Kayleigh was a "vulnerable adult".

I'd laughed, after a beat, and told them that the only other person living in Kayleigh's building was a loser who's got nothing better to do than dye his hair all day, who'd been in love with Kayleigh for years – love which was obviously unrequited – and he was jealous of mine and Kayleigh's relationship. And the fact he wasn't the father of her kid. I let the implication that I was Liam's father just hang there. If they thought I was, that was up to them. I admitted that Kayleigh and I had had a few arguments recently, and said we were both tired, what with the new baby and everything. I saw an opportunity. I said that Kayleigh was bipolar and that she hadn't been taking her meds, and only yesterday I'd had to call her psychiatrist because I was worried about her mental health. I told them I'd had to restrain her on several occasions for her own safety, and that was what the "member of the public" must have heard.

When I'd finished, the pigs glanced at each other and nodded. The bloke said they were going to take no further action, but the complaint and this conversation would be logged.

I finished my coffee, relieved, because I'd blagged it with the pigs, livid with that twat, Will, and ecstatic, because now I knew how to fuck Kayleigh up.

Kayleigh

When Rich stormed out of my flat after our argument I was elated. There was no other word for it. He'd threatened me, but what the fuck could he do, really? He'd done everything but kill me, and I was still standing, and Liam was happy and healthy, and still asleep in his Moses basket. I thought about having a nap myself. I really needed some rest. I stripped down to my vest top and underwear and got into bed. My foot started jiggling almost immediately. I pulled the duvet more tightly around me, and closed my eyes, but they sprang open again, and I had an overwhelming urge to clean the flat and get my life organised. Both the health visitor and Lucy from the Perinatal Team had advised me to sleep when Liam slept and to "bugger the housework", so I tried to do the breathing exercises that one of the psychologists from Dr Whittle's team had suggested for me. But it was useless. I couldn't concentrate. That's why I'd never got into yoga or any of that crap. I couldn't focus for two minutes, let alone half an hour. Still, I decided to be a good girl and try to get the rest I needed in order to look after Liam properly. So I opened the bottle of cab sav that Rich had left on the side – red wine always made me sleepy – poured myself a little glass and took it back to bed. I couldn't down it like I had when I was younger, so I rummaged in my bedside cabinet, and pulled out my Book of Shadows. I'd flip through it while I was waiting for the tiredness to hit. I hadn't looked at it in years. I'd like to be able to say that it was a gilt-edged, leather-bound tome that wouldn't look out of place in a university library. But I wasn't Cath. My Book of Shadows was just a few reporter notebooks from WHSmith that I'd linked together with green pipe cleaners. My intention had been to just flip through, but I was soon absorbed. It was like I was becoming Kayleigh again – the one I had been before all of the craziness started. It felt like coming home. I was ecstatic – reading, making notes, chanting, pulling all my old books out from where I'd stashed them away, in binbags, under my bed. I arrived in the front room, flung open the curtains and the window, and flipped off the lights. The moon was full, of course it was, and it provided all the light I needed. I took off the rest of my clothes. I felt pure and, using my Book of Shadows, I performed a full moon ritual, after which I realised that all the wine had gone. Panicking because I didn't want to lose this feeling, I ransacked my flat for alcohol, and found an unopened bottle of Mad Dog 20/20 in a rucksack Rich had left in my wardrobe, and I had some straight from the bottle to save on washing up, and realised I hadn't done a naming ceremony for Liam, what with everything. And then something urged me to look out of the window.

It was the same feeling I'd got when I sat down opposite Dr Grosvenor – visceral fear. So, kneeling on the carpet, and putting my head level with the inside of the window, I looked out. Just passing the phone box and heading towards the church was Rich. He could only be coming here. I was under attack from psychic vampires! I had to defend myself and my son. Very aware that I was naked now, I grabbed my books. I'd never had to repel a psychic attack before, but I needed to now – right now. The day wasn't right, the moon wasn't right, so I did what I could – I lit a half-burnt joss stick that was still in its holder on the coffee table, grabbed my black candle and lit that too, tore Cath's ring from the chain around my neck and passed it through the smoke and the flame, and then – I don't know why, but it felt like a good thing to do – I seized my ceremonial knife and drew it over the faint white scar on my wrist. I bled, and I held the ring under the drips, recited the words, and put the ring on the only finger I could get it on – the little finger of my left hand. I'd just forced it over my finger joint when there was an almighty bang on the door. I ran to check Liam, who had stirred but that was all, and I ran out of my flat and down to the front door, chanting over and over, and Rich was shouting as well as banging now. I wrenched the door open and screamed the words in his face – "All doors are barred on all the planes! No way is found to enter here! All evil returns unto the sender! I live my life in joy, not fear!" Rich laughed, and tried to push me back into the house, but I was screaming, "All doors are barred –"

I punched him hard in the chest with both hands, and some of my blood had splashed onto his face and his white T-shirt, and I realised I was still clutching the knife, and then Will appeared on the path behind Rich, coming home from the Riverboat, smoking a really long rolly – why do I remember that? – and he was trying to put his coat around me and get me to give him the knife. I said I'm not the murderer, Rich is. And Rich was saying I'm a danger to his child, and I said Liam is not your child and you're a vampire, and we were all shouting, really, and then Will got the knife out of my hand and I didn't know where it went, and he was running back up the road and went in the phone box, and I was still demanding of Rich why he said that about Liam when it wasn't true. And some of the people had come out of their houses. Then I heard sirens and a police officer with long dark hair was saying she had a warrant and was telling me to calm down or she'd have to detain me, and I didn't understand and I was cold, but I had Will's coat on now, and I wished I hadn't been drinking and knew I had to check on Liam, and the officer was asking me really nicely to come with her. But I said no way, I had to protect my son and Rich was the murderer. But he was saying he was my nearest relative and Will was saying what's your mum's phone number, and Rich was laughing, and looking at something on the floor but I saw it too and made a grab for it and I was running back inside with the knife so Rich couldn't get it and hurt Liam, but the police were just behind me and got me on the stairs and there was a paramedic, and the lady was saying are you refusing and I said too fucking right I'm refusing, I've done nothing wrong, and she spun me around and put handcuffs on me and said she was detaining me under

Section Four and was taking me to a place of safety, and Liam would be fine, and then I saw Liam's fluffy T-Rex on the floor and I asked her to pick it up and she looked at me for a second and then she did, and I was in the police car, and the last thing I remember were two people staring at me through the glass: Richard laughing and Will with tears streaming down his face, like that pair of theatre masks.

Richard

My work there was nearly done.

A couple of days later I'd handed in my notice at Tesco and put my flat on the market. There was no point staying in this backwater any longer and turning into one of them. Cath was dead, Adam had seen sense and left town, and Kayleigh, the slut, was in the loony-bin, where she belonged. No doubt her son, a bastard in every sense of the word would end up in care. My half of Nan's inheritance was still pretty substantial (I was still waiting for Adam's cheque to clear, but I had no concerns that it wouldn't) so I'd thought about moving right away and starting up again. And as Cath hadn't made it to Manchester, I thought I'd try there. I could try to get into the university. The irony of it made me smile. Maybe I'd bump into that Gallagher twat and fuck him up too. But the fire wasn't there any more. I was tired. I couldn't be bothered with work today. I finished placing my orders, walked over to Wyman's office, and asked him if I could take a half-day. The sun was shining, and I thought I'd drive down to Lyme Regis, buy some chips and eat them on the sea front, and go for a walk along the beach and the cliffs to see if I could find any fossils. I'd be happy with an ammonite. My mind was wandering, and I thought if I ever had a daughter I'd call her Mary-Anne, after Mary Anning. I pulled my jacket out of my locker and zipped it up over my uniform so I wouldn't get bothered by customers when I got back onto the shop floor. I felt calm, which was weird. Maybe this was what closure felt like.

The automatic doors had just registered and opened for me, when in strode Keith. He clocked me immediately, stormed over, and shoved me back with both hands.

"You miserable little fuck!" he shouted. I put my hands up in mock surrender and laughed.

"Have you gone crazy, old man?!" People had stopped to look at us, and the big guys on security were watching intently. There was a new bloke on the team today, and he was staring daggers at me.

"You put that poor girl in hospital! She might lose her son! Do you have any idea what you've done?! She could lose her son because of you!" Keith pushed me again. He was stronger than he looked. The security veterans thought they'd let the rookie sort it out so, after a moment's hesitation, the new bloke stomped over and put a heavy hand on Keith's shoulder.

"Sorry, mate. Not in here," he said. "I'm afraid I'm going to have to ask you to leave." I read his name badge and almost pissed myself with laughter. The new bloke was Andy from school! Bloody hell, he'd put some weight on. But then I guess he'd had to give up football.

I smiled and raised my eyebrows. "Hi, Andy – long time no see! Can you get this old bastard out of my face, please? I don't know him and I haven't got a fucking clue what he's on about," I said, smirking.

Keith glared at me. He gave me a look so full of hate, it felt like I'd been shot. Andy just stood there, staring at me, his fists clenched, torn between wanting to kick my head in, and wanting to keep his new job. Keith stepped towards me. "Andy!" one of his security team shouted. "Get the old guy out of here!" Spineless fucker that he was, Andy put his hands on Keith's shoulders, turned him round, and escorted him through the doors. Then Keith stopped walking and twisted his head round to look at me.

"You clear this mess up, son," he said.

"I'm no son of yours, old man!" I retorted.

Keith laughed, and the sound was hollow. "Actually, yes, you are."

Kayleigh

I wonder how my mum feels. I've never questioned her motives before. I just presumed that she cared more for her new bloke than for me. I'd heard her crying down the phone to one of her friends before, telling her she felt like I was her jailer more than her daughter. She must have felt a wrench, though, to actually leave me down here in the West Country and move back up north. Back home. I know I was an adult, and had a flat and a job by then, but it still can't have been easy for her. I can see that now, after having had Liam. I think the trouble was, I saw her as a kind of God. As if people just turned into grown-ups and all the answers fell into their laps. When I realised I was pregnant, I thought I'd just 'turn into' a mum, like a butterfly emerging from its chrysalis, and I was shocked when I found I was still me. I still had my life to live. I was still 'Kayleigh', with all her confusion and foibles and insecurities. I thought I'd just be 'Liam's Mum', and turn into a kind of walking placenta, existing only to raise my son. But I didn't. I was still me. It was a revelation. My parents were actually still individuals, just trying to do their best for themselves and for me. I felt bad for all the times I'd slagged them off.

What I'm feeling is so deep and primal that I'm sure it must be innate in all mothers. I've been sitting here on the bed for days, and it's almost like I have a fever. I get rushes of anguish so intense that they've cut my nails because I've scratched myself so badly in the act of trying to tear my heart out. They keep me sedated, so I get periods of quiet where I'm just still and numb, but the anguish returns. They check on me every fifteen minutes when I'm in my room, lifting the flap on the grill over my door. It's like I'm in custody. I'm

172

trying to contain my emotions, because, through the fog of whatever sedative they're giving me, I'm aware I need to cooperate if I'm going to get out of here. But they've taken my boy. It's like my heart has been ripped out. There aren't words for the depth of emotion I'm feeling.

Apparently they can keep me here for seventy-two hours while they "get things sorted out". When I refused a sedative, they gave me one intravenously. I'm taking tablets now. There's no point arguing. They can do what they like. They said I can appeal, but how the fuck can I do that? They'd spoken to Dr Grosvenor, Perinatal Lucy, someone called Phoenix Canonteign, and my own doctor, Dr Farefield. Apparently, they'd had several phone calls from people "close to me" who were concerned for my mental health. They were very nice about it all. Apparently I am ill and delusional and they have a duty to protect me, my son and other members of the public. And they've given me olanzapine on top of my lithium and the sedative.

Eventually, inevitably, I'd start crying. The nurses would tell me, gently, that Liam was safe, that I was ill, and that I needed to get better in order to look after him properly again. And, for a minute, I'd believe them, and take the plastic mug of warm decaf tea they'd offer me. I'd been allowed to keep Liam's T-Rex with me because, I supposed, if it was safe enough for a baby then it was safe enough for a schizophrenic. Yeah, schizophrenic. Apparently, there had been debate as to whether I was 'bipolar 1 with psychotic symptoms', but Dr Whittle was 'unavailable' so that new psychiatrist-vampire Dr Grosvenor had stepped in and changed my diagnosis.

I had to queue up to get my meds every morning and evening. There were six of us on the Acute Admissions Unit, and we all had to take pills twice a day.

We'd be in a line outside a big room that was lit up like a supermarket, and was only open – that I saw – at med times. It had no windows and it was full of locked cupboards. Four nurses stood up against these cupboards and another sat on one of the two stools that were fixed to the floor in the

173

middle of the room. The nurse on the door, as it were, who was in charge of the line, let us in one at a time. Once inside, the door was closed. We had to sit on the free stool, and the nurse on the other stool would count our meds out into a transparent plastic shot glass. One of the other nurses would name the drug, and the strength and quantity of tablets, and mark it off on a chart in a red folder. The shot glass would be handed to us, and we'd be asked to take our pills, one at a time. We'd be given a plastic cup which was half-full of water, to swallow them with, and after each pill, the nurse on the stool next to us would ask us to open our mouths, and she'd check in our cheeks and under our tongues to make sure we'd swallowed the pills. Then we'd be escorted back to the door and, once outside, would be free to go.

'Free'. Stupid word to use. All but one of us on the ward had been sectioned. Most of us would talk to each other when we were let into the garden to have a cigarette (those of us who were allowed to smoke). The garden was secure, of course, like the rest of the unit - a scarily tall, metal, mesh fence, ran around the perimeter. I remember thinking that it was topped with barbed wire, but my memories aren't clear, and my distance vision isn't brilliant, so maybe it wasn't. It felt like it was, at any rate.

We'd sit on the smooth wooden benches and pretend we couldn't see the nurses who were supervising us. Chat was hesitant at first, but there's a need in most humans to connect – or at least fill a silence – and we'd talk and smoke quietly.

In my more lucid moments I found it all quite interesting and thanked the Goddess for this insight into a world that the majority of people (thankfully) don't see. We are the one-in-fours.

Today I sat in the sunshine and stretched out my legs. We were all dressed in soft pyjamas and cordless dressing gowns, as if we were on some fucked up sleep-over – and I watched my grey-clad arms and legs sweep back and forth through the soft, green plants. (The softness of the plants and the clothes were incongruous with the fence, but I guess that's life.) Vera, the old lady who'd been in and out of here a lot, said

174

she'd tried eating the plants in the hopes that they were poisonous. But she'd been caught mid-mouthful, and told that, of course, they were not.

As well as Vera and me, there was an unageable bloke who thought he was Ronnie O'Sullivan, a loud fat girl, with what was once pillar-box-red hair, but who had been here so long she had four inches of mousy roots (she had bandaged wrists, and always wore sleeveless tops so everyone could see how badly she'd sliced up her arms). There was a skinny bloke too, with long stubble and shaggy black hair, who spent all day curled up in 'his' armchair in the TV room, and finally there was Lizzie, the voluntary patient, who was really quite sane, but had randomly taken an overdose of sertraline. I say 'sane' like I say 'voluntary'. One day we were sitting there in the garden, and suddenly she stubbed out her cigarette, and ran and jumped at the fence. She tried to scramble up it, but a nurse managed to grab her foot. Lizzie kicked, and her regulation slipper came off, and she somehow scrambled to the top! But they got her down, of course they did. Her hands were all cut from pulling herself up the metal fence as quickly as she could. She got moved. She wasn't voluntary after that.

The slipper stayed where it had fallen in the bushes for days, like a warning. It was worse than a head on a spike. I heeded it, and gained some control over myself, although I still couldn't stomach food. I was in the TV room one day, with the silent bloke, when a nurse came in, told me that I had a visitor, and asked if I'd like to see him. I was so taken aback that I nearly spilled my tea. I had to go to the canteen – a place I rarely frequented – where visitors were allowed, and was overjoyed to see Will's battered denim jacket hanging over one of the chairs.

"Will!" I ran over to him in as straight a line as I was able and hugged him so hard that he laughed. He hugged me back, and we stayed like that for some time, until I realised I was crying.

Will finished making his tea and then guided me over to the chair on which his jacket hung, and I tried to ask him so many questions, and was crying so hard that all I did was pull a load of stupid faces. I was simultaneously acutely aware that I hadn't been allowed to shave, file my nails, or pluck my eyebrows while I'd been in here. As I couldn't get a word out, Will said, "It's okay, Kayleigh. I was there when they took you in. I've spoken to the doctors and called your mum. Dr Whittle's coming in sometime to assess you. Your mum's staying at your flat, and she's got Liam. Don't worry. He won't go into care. You won't lose him." Then he pulled me close, and I dissolved into tears again.

When I collapsed into bed at 9.30 p.m., I was smiling with relief. I clutched Liam's T-Rex close and whispered *Where the Wild Things Are* in its ear, as I had done every night I'd been in here. But tonight I did it with hope in my heart.

Richard

It's a wonder that I didn't kill anyone as I drove to Lyme Regis – accidentally, or on purpose.

Instinctively I'd known that the old man's words were true. In spite of that, I'd stood there, inside the automatic doors, with my bloody mouth open, as shoppers either stopped to stare at me, or rubbernecked as they walked by with baskets and trolleys. Andy had waited on the pavement to make sure Keith had walked away. I'd been aware some of the bastards I worked with were staring too. Everyone in this shithole of a town would know by tea-time. Pride eventually kicked in and I laughed, shook my head, and walked out. Andy caught my arm as I passed him. "One day you'll get yours," he hissed, and spat in my face. I laughed, kicked his leg, and strode off.

I didn't turn my head or my gaze until I got in my car. It was parked, as it always was, in the garage at the end of the courtyard that lay behind the double wooden doors next to the door to my flat. It was a black BMW 3 Series, and it was my pride and joy. I didn't even go upstairs and change out of my uniform. I got into the car, wheel-span the thing out onto the road, and punched the button on the tape deck. I didn't stop to get out and shut the garage doors. I just burnt up the hill, past the big church, the swimming pool, and the school, heading for the motorway. I blasted down the M5 until I got to Junction 30. I turned off and headed east to Lyme Regis. I played the music loud, and just kept turning the tape over. I didn't let myself think until I realised that I was crying and was finding it hard to see. I pulled in to the first car park in Lyme Regis I came to, cutting up a load of cyclists in the process. And that's when it hit me – Keith must have bought me that bike I covered in dinosaur stickers when I was a kid; fuck me, he'd taught me how to ride!

There was a tap at the window. A woman with long, dark hair, was peering in at me with a concerned expression. I took my forehead off the steering wheel and met her eyes.

"Mr Morrell? Mr Morrell, are you all right?" Her voice was muffled, coming through the glass, but her enunciation had been exaggerated. I wound down the window.

"How do you know my name?"

The woman straightened up so I could see her uniform.

"Step out of the car, please, sir," she said.

"What?" I just looked at the dark-haired pig and laughed.

"Now, please, sir."

"What the FUCKING HELL is going on?" I demanded, punching the steering wheel with both fists before I acquiesced. Then I noticed the other police car behind her, and her stern-looking musclehead of a colleague, who was staring at me, with his meaty hand on its roof.

"Richard Morrell, I'm arresting you –"

"You what?!"

"– for the murder of Catherine Lock –"

"What the fuck?!"

She had her hands on my shoulders, trying to twist me around, and something in her right hand glinted silver – handcuffs. I saw my fists punch her in the chest. She stumbled backwards onto the tarmac looking so shocked that I laughed, but the musclehead was running over, so I kicked her in the face with my steel toecaps, heard the crunch, and ran.

I had no idea where I was, so I just ran full-pelt downhill, in what I hoped must be the direction of the sea. I'd hoped the second pig would stop to help his colleague. That was the main reason I kicked her. But he hadn't. I heard his heavy footsteps thudding against the tarmac behind me. He was fitter than I'd thought. I heard him shouting, presumably down his radio, and I cursed myself for smoking so much. I had to get to the sea – preferably off a cliff – but I'd run in if

I had to, and keep running until it was over. I imagined my body eventually sinking, rotting on the sea floor, my skeleton resting quietly in the darkness with the fossils, where it belonged, where it had come from, where all life had originated. There was no mysteriously moving God, and there was no Selenophile Goddess. They were human constructs to comfort the weak – life was chance, survival of the fittest – you had to look after number one –

The ground levelled out – I saw the sea – a quaint little harbour – yellow sand with a low, grey wall around it – I could have sat on it and eaten my chips – where were the cliffs? I slowed down to look around me – I saw a sign for the museum and wondered if it was open – the sand was absorbing my pace – the pig was shouting, some blokes were running – the shock of the cold water through my work trousers and finally in my shoes – I was waist-deep, but they were on me – if I could just get my head under the water and inhale – I could taste the salt, but arms stronger than mine were around my middle, pulling me back – I kept lunging forward, I had to get under the water, just for a few seconds – but I couldn't get my breath, I didn't have the strength – I was so tired –

I was on my side on the wet sand. There were hands on me, but without pressure: we all knew I was going nowhere. I felt the surf on my ankle. I could see the cliffs. I smiled.

"… you do not have to say anything, but … " and the rest was a blur. I stared out of the window in the back of the police car, wrapped in a blanket. Some brine dripped from my hair, and I put my tongue out to catch it. I tasted the salt, and my overriding feeling was that I was pissed off I hadn't even got my chips.

They put me in a kind of glass cubicle and took my wallet, jacket and shoes off me. Then I was escorted by the two of them down a long corridor until we arrived at the cell I'd been allocated. I could hear the other blokes who were on remand banging on their iron doors, shouting. I think I was in denial, because I still didn't believe this was happening. As a

179

result I kept laughing, which obviously didn't endear me to the pigs.

"She slashed her wrists! How the fuck can you arrest someone for murder when the person who's dead blatantly killed themselves?! This is bullshit!"

One of the pigs wrenched open a heavy, blue door, and held it open for me.

"Make yourself comfortable, Mr Morrell," he said.

I laughed again and looked him I the face as I stepped into the cell. "Fuck you."

I sauntered across the windowless square and plonked myself down on the low blue bench that ran halfway around the room like a dado rail. There was a seatless, steel toilet in one corner, but there was no loo roll. In the opposite corner was a white, crocheted blanket – presumably for me to sleep under. It didn't enter my mind for a minute that I'd actually need to use it.

Catherine's Novel

I feel tiny, invisible. People bump into me when I walk down the street, even if I am the only other person on the pavement. When I talk to Luke, I often have to repeat myself because he doesn't hear me at first. He's preoccupied, and I wonder if he's planning to kill me. I was staying at his flat the other night – primarily because I couldn't bear to be in my parents' company, pretending to watch the telly all evening again – and I was in the kitchen doing a stir-fry while he was slumped in the armchair, flicking through the Gazette.

Suddenly he stood up and announced, "I'm going out."

"What?! Why? Dinner will be ready in literally a minute!"

"Yeah, I won't be long," he said as he disappeared down the stairs. He hadn't even looked at me.

I turned down the heat and got the plates and cutlery out. Then I poured myself a large glass of wine. I crossed into the front room and picked the Gazette up off the floor where Luke had dropped it. I started flicking through it myself. He said he wouldn't be long. After ten minutes I took the food off the heat and covered the pan with a plate. I was hungry, but I was scared he'd get angry if I started eating without him. I put the telly on and finished my wine. It was nasty – a buy-one-get-one-free bottle from the corner shop at the end of the road. I started cleaning up, glancing at the kitchen clock as I plugged the hoover in. He'd been gone an hour-and-a-half. I hoovered the whole flat, including going in the corners with the pipes. Then I cleaned the kitchen and the bathroom. I knew Luke would be in the Barge, but what was I going to do - go down there and demand he came home for his dinner? I felt a whole load of emotions. I was angry,

181

humiliated and scared. I wanted to scream at him, but most of all I just longed for him to come back up the stairs and apologise, and just hold me. I knew that wasn't going to happen.

It occurred to me that I ought to stop drinking, but I finished what was left in the bottle, and opened a new one. I'd begun to love that glug you get when you pour the first glass of a new bottle. I turned the telly off and put a CD on, loud. Dad had given me *The Bends* by Radiohead for Christmas. Well, it was supposedly from him and Mum, but Mum had never had a clue about music. I knew that if I called my parents, one of them would come and get me, or I could walk home and never come back here, and go to university like they wanted, and forget about it all. But I was scared, and somehow I couldn't leave. Also, some fucked up part of me wanted to see what would happen.

I played *High and Dry* on repeat until well after midnight, just lying on the sofa under a blanket, intermittently sitting up to glug some wine. I had no idea what I was going to say when Luke turned up. If he turned up.

Eventually I got cold and uncomfortable and went to bed, taking the dregs of the wine with me. I left the food covered by the plate next to the cooker, and the cutlery and crockery laid out ready on the table.

I woke when the front door slammed, and opened my eyes to darkness. I turned my head so that I could see the digital alarm clock-radio on the bedside table. It was quarter past three in the morning. I heard Luke stumbling up the stairs, and I lay in the blackness, my heart racing. The kitchen light clicked on, and I heard him laugh. Luke poured himself a pint of water, as he habitually did after a night out, in the hope that it would stop him getting a hangover. Then he went in the bathroom.

'Thank God,' I thought. Recently he'd been coming home so wrecked that he'd pissed in the wardrobe and up the radiator, and I'd had to clean it up at stupid o'clock in the morning when I had to get up for work soon. He thought this was really funny, and I'd heard him laughing about it with his friends. They thought it was funny, too. I sometimes wonder if I am actually the sane one.

The bathroom light went off, and Luke lurched into the bedroom. The main light went on, and I winced at the sudden brightness.

"Oh, sorry, love," Luke slurred. He leant back on the wall and pulled his shoes and jeans off. "I'm sorry," he said. His speech was thick, and I could smell the alcohol on him, even from over there. He crawled up the bed from its foot and lay down beside me. He didn't so much cuddle me as let his arm fall across my chest. "I'm cold," he said after a while, and manoeuvred himself under the quilt, pressing himself against me. Then he slurred in my ear, "I'd like to fuck you now, Lola."

And I let him.

Kayleigh

I dared to hope that Dr Whittle would be knocking on my door at the crack of dawn with a big smile, itching to un-section me. Even though I knew in my heart that it was an unrealistic dream, I was still disappointed when I sat down in the canteen with my plastic mug of warm tea at 11 a.m. One of the nurses told me he was still working his way through his ward-round.

I wandered into the TV lounge and lay on my back on the sofa. Matey with all the hair was in there, as ever, in silence, crunched up in his armchair. I wondered if he'd get thrombosis. Images flashed across the screen, but I didn't register what the programmes were. I shut my eyes and soon the crazy thoughts came, and I knew I was falling asleep.

Someone was shaking my shoulder. "Kayleigh?" I jumped a bit, opened my eyes, and turned my head. "Kayleigh? Your friend, Will, is here to see you."

Still in a bit of a fog, I made my way into the canteen. Will stood up when he saw me, a big smile on his face, and hugged me. I was happy to see him, but I would have been happier if he'd been Dr Whittle. The disappointment must have shown on my face because Will said, "I'm sorry you're still in here, Kayleigh. We'll get you out – don't worry!" and he hugged me again.

We sat at one of the round tables. Will had already got two mugs of tepid tea, so I took one, not caring if it had a hundred sugars in it, and cradled it in my hands, wishing it was warmer.

"Kayleigh, we've found something."

I looked at Will expectantly.

"Cath was in the middle of writing a novel."

"Yes, I know," I said, disappointment flooding my senses again. "She was always writing something. I take it you found it. Did you read it?"

"It wasn't hard to find. It was in the top drawer of her desk. I thought it was her actual diary at first, and I felt a bit dodgy about reading it, but I knew I had to, so I did. And when I picked it up, it was an actual diary. Sorry, that's confusing. I mean the ones like books that you can buy in WHSmith. There were loads more underneath it, all with 1998 on, and she'd basically written her novel in them. Well, I say it was a novel – the names were different, but you could tell who the people were. I haven't finished it yet, but, Christ, some of the things Rich did to her were unbelievable. If what she wrote was true. Everything else was, so I can't see why she'd make up that, but –"

"Oh my God, I knew it!" I said, my eyes watering. "Poor Cath. Why didn't she ever talk about anything?" Again, I got the terrible feeling I'd let her down. I'd been such a shit friend. I started to cry. "Have you given it to the police?" I whispered through the tears.

"That's the thing, Kayleigh. There's no proof that any of it's true. It's just stuff written in a diary that reads like a diary, but is supposed to be a novel. If we ever get Rich to court, the defence would dismiss it. At the very most, they'd say she was a mentally ill, vindictive girlfriend. Your mum's gone to Land and Underhill today for some legal advice."

"Who's looking after Liam?" I suddenly panicked. Why hadn't I asked about him earlier? I was a shit friend and a shit mum.

"It's okay. Cath's mum and dad have got him for the day." He searched my expression. "Kayleigh, he's fine, honestly. He clearly misses you, but he's quite a laid-back kid, and he settles down. And he's got his cow – the one you can hang off things – although I can't find his T-Rex –" Will got up and hugged me where I sat in the chair. I was in floods of tears now and held on to Will's shoulders to stop myself from falling. We stayed like that for a long time, until I stopped crying, and until my breathing returned to normal. My brain

185

started making crazy leaps, and I felt like I was falling asleep again. Suddenly, it was clear. If Rich hadn't actually slashed Cath's wrists, he'd either literally or metaphorically put the razor in her hand. I had to get out of there, had to speak to the police and the solicitors. Rich had killed my best friend, and I would prove it.

And then something else hit me. I knew about the rape, but who was going to believe a schizophrenic in a psychiatric hospital under a section? They'd say I was delusional. The fucking murdering bastard knew that I knew and had me sectioned to shut me up!

"Kayleigh, what's wrong?" Will had felt me tense up and had pulled away. My blood was running cold, and I could see from my hands that all of the colour had drained out of me. I had to be so careful now. Every fibre of my body wanted to scream that Rich had done this to me, and had taken my little boy away from me, but I knew that if I did that, I would look like I was psychotic, and they'd sedate me, and I'd never get out – with or without Dr Whittle. And how come he was back all of a sudden? Thank the Goddess for Will. I held on to his shoulders and whispered in his ear. We stared at each other in silence, while all the hurt, anger and hatred boiled in our eyes. And that crazy part of my brain went off again, and I thought, 'All these years and I never knew Will had any fire inside of him. Until now.'

Richard

Fuck knows how long I'd been in the cell, if that's what it was called. Was this custody? They hadn't charged me. There were no windows, and the harsh light in the ceiling never went out, so I'd lost all track of time. I couldn't work out if it was day, night, the same day I'd been taken in, or three weeks later. I'd been offered food and drink, and although I drank the tea, I'd refused all the food because I had no appetite. I realised that I ought to eat, but – and I'd admitted this to myself – I was too scared to stomach anything, so I sat on the bench with my head in my hands for a bit, and then gave up, crawled under the blanket, and tried to get some sleep.

The door clanged open.

"Mr Morrell?"

"Yes?" I said, sitting bolt upright, suddenly alert.

"Follow me, please," the pig said. "It's time for your interview."

I needed a piss, but I couldn't risk being in there any longer than absolutely necessary, so I followed her. She was short, blonde, and built like a brick shithouse. If she'd had an anchor tattoo, it wouldn't have surprised me. She'd cuffed me again before she led me out of my cell, back along the corridor, and into a friendlier-looking part of the building. It had carpet, paint and wooden doors.

The blonde pig opened a numbered door on to another windowless, square room. I shivered, suddenly panicking that I'd never see the sky again. Shit – I was losing my nerve. I told myself that they had nothing on me: Cath had slit her wrists, for fuck's sake!

I sat on one of the chairs on the far side of the interview

table. How many times had I seen a set-up like this on TV? I shook my head in disbelief that this was happening, and sat back, trying to appear relaxed and confident in the chair, with my left ankle on my right knee, and my arms crossed. I was pissed off they'd managed to scare me.

The door was closed on me, and I sat there alone, smiling because I knew they were trying to intimidate me, and it wasn't going to work.

After a while two different pigs came in, followed by a bloke who wasn't my solicitor, but who sat down next to me anyway.

"Who the fuck are you?" I demanded.

"I'm going to represent you, Mr Morrell. We'll talk together after this interview – through which I'll advise you."

"No we won't, *mate*," I said. "Where's the bloke from Land and Underhill?"

"I'll be representing you instead, Mr Morrell. For now I'd advise you not to answer any questions other than to confirm your name and address." He sounded bored. He'd been here a thousand times.

"What the fuck?! This is bullshit!"

One of the pigs cut in. "Mr Morrell – can I call you Richard? – Fine. When did you first meet Catherine Lock, Mr Morrell?"

I answered without thinking – "About a year ago, in Tesco. Why? Why are you bothering with this charade when we all know she killed herself?"

The officer ignored my question.

"No, Mr Morrell. When did you first meet her? It was more like seven years ago wasn't it? When Catherine was just thirteen."

Kayleigh

It was three days later when a nurse came and found me and said that it was time for my assessment with Dr Whittle. I'd given up hope by then. I was on my bed, in the foetal position, hugging Liam's T-Rex toy. I'd cried myself out by then, but I hadn't bothered showering or eating that day. I knew I looked a mess, and that it wasn't going to work in my favour. I sat up, angry at myself, and projected it onto my psychiatrist.

I followed the nurse up to the office that was usually closed. She opened the door onto a rectangular room which had watercolours of deer in woods and fields hanging on the walls and a thick red and blue patterned carpet. It reminded me of the front bar of the Riverboat, and I stifled a sudden urge to laugh. Directly opposite the door was a large window, and the sun was streaming through it, casting the person who was sitting in the chair in front of it into shadow. Chairs ran down the other sides of the room and on them sat a police officer, some of the nurses on the ward, my midwife, Perinatal Lucy, a dishevelled lady who turned out to be a social worker, a thin lady with spectacular earrings who was introduced as Phoenix Canonteign, and someone who I think used to work at the solicitors with Cath. I wondered briefly what she was doing here, but then my eyes fell on Will, who was smiling up at me. I immediately felt better and sat down in the seat next to him, which had clearly been left empty for me. The nurse I had followed up to the room came in, closed the door behind her and stood with her back to it, and I realised I was on trial.

As I sat down, the person on the chair in front of the window stood up. Of course, it was Dr Whittle. He smiled at me like an old friend, then checked himself and said, "Hello, Kayleigh." He sat back down, heavily. He looked tired.

"Where've you been?" I asked, trying not to swear or snap at him. "Where's Dr Grosvenor?" Will sensed the tension in my tone and took my hand. I was vaguely aware that it was unwashed and clammy.

Dr Whittle crossed his legs and put on a kind, professional smile. "I'm sorry I've been unavailable until now, Kayleigh," he said. He let the apology hang in the air – it was clear he wasn't going to offer any kind of explanation. After an awkward pause he continued. "Today we're going to assess your current psychiatric condition with a view to releasing you from hospital. I've a feeling, just looking at you, that the outcome is going to be favourable, but there is a process that has to be followed, especially where there is a child involved."

I was getting out of here! I was going to see Liam again! But I was torn. I didn't want to jeopardise my future with Liam, but I'd been lucky, and I felt that in return for that I should do what was morally right and try to get justice for my friend. I should rid the world of an evil at the same time. I had to tell Dr Whittle what I'd remembered; maybe the Three Fold Law would kick in. But what if they thought I was mad again?

At the end of the meeting it was obvious I should leave the room first. They were all looking at me, smiling expectantly, in a thank-you-we're-all-pleased-for-you-but-we-need-to-discuss-you-in-private kind of way. But I hesitated. "Dr Whittle, would it be possible to talk to you alone for a moment?" I asked.

It was like I'd shot him. The colour drained out of Dr Whittle's face, the eyes of everyone else in the room flew to him and then back to me. "It's – I've – something happened to me, years ago, and – I need to tell someone."

Dr Whittle recovered himself. "I think that under the circumstances, Kayleigh, if you have anything you want to tell me regarding your illness, it would be best for you to share it with all of us here. If you feel you are able to, of course."

Will stared me in the face, obviously confused and concerned. I reached out and put my hand over his clenched fist, and I told them about the night I was raped and about what had exploded into my head the morning after. I told them it was like I'd lived that Halloween night again, that I didn't know why I'd suddenly remembered after all this time, that I thought Cath had been raped after Rich had knocked me out. I started to cry and said, "I don't know what's happening to me, but I'm not mad. And please, I'm begging you, don't take Liam away from me –" and Will got off his chair, knelt in front of me, and wrapped his arms around me.

When I had calmed down a bit, Will moved back onto his seat, but he kept his arm around me. His face was like stone, unreadable. Then Dr Whittle uncrossed and re-crossed his legs, smiled sympathetically, and said, "Kayleigh, I am very glad that you have been able to tell us this today. What you experienced is called a 'flashback'. It is common for people who have suffered trauma to suppress their memory of it. Sometimes when people drink a lot of alcohol, they know what is happening to them at the time, but the next day they can't remember anything. Often the memory of it comes back to them in full or in part, in a few hours, or days – but sometimes it doesn't come back at all. In sufferers of trauma it is similar. Some people regain the memory of what happened after a while. Sometimes, as in your case, years later. And some don't. I wonder if you would consider talking to my colleague Phoenix Canonteign about it as part of your Care Plan –" I cut him off. Tears were streaming down my face again.

"Could the same thing have happened to Cath?"

I'd been to the trial, obviously, so I knew the outcome. But I didn't let myself believe it until I saw it on the breakfast news.

Liam still wasn't walking yet, but he liked to pull himself up, and to lean on the coffee table to watch the telly. He also liked to flip the channels with the remote, and that's how we got from *Babar* to the local BBC news. Mum and I were sitting on the sofa drinking coffee and eating peanut butter on toast. I was breaking off pieces to give to Liam and he loved it, so I was happy, even though he left sticky fingerprints all over the glass top of the coffee table. Mum had decided to stay and help for a while, and it was actually lovely having her here, not just for the help with Liam and the company, but because it was her. And I'd missed my mum. We'd talked a lot about her and Dad's divorce, the reasons why she moved away. And I told her about Liam's dad. Mum adored Liam, and she even laughed when he put his hands in a newly opened yoghurt pot, pulled them out, and clapped, spraying yoghurt everywhere.

And then we heard Rich's name and watched the telly.

"... Richard Morrell, who is 36, and from Devon, was convicted of manslaughter, following the death of 20-year-old student and promising writer, Catherine Lock, and the rape of a 21-year-old woman, also from Devon ... "

The TV showed Rich, head bent and partially covered by a towel, being rushed into a police van.

"You were very brave, love," said Mum, patting my knee, "Speaking up, going through all that – and what they said about the state of Cath's body. I – I'm just so sorry –" and she broke off before the tears came again.

I smiled at her and picked up Liam, who had collapsed onto his bum, and was still reaching for the remote. I sat back down on the sofa, kissed his yellow, curly hair, and gave him a cuddle.

The phone rang and Mum got up, put her coffee on the table, and went into the hall to answer it. Liam was gabbling, pulling my hair over my eyes and back again, laughing.

"Kayleigh, it's for you, love," she shouted from where she stood in the hall.

I put Liam in Mum's arms and she bounced him over to the window to watch a flock of jackdaws that were cawing loudly on a neighbour's lawn.

"Hello?" I pulled the telephone cord as far as it would

reach, so I could watch Mum and Liam.

"Kayleigh?"

I froze.

"Kayleigh?"

"Yes. Adam –" I whispered. My legs felt like jelly.

"Kayleigh, I'm so sorry. So, so fucking sorry –"

"It's okay," I said, automatically. And it was.

"Kayleigh, I want to come back. I need to see our son. Is there any chance I –"

"Yes," I said.

I was smiling so widely when I floated back into the living room that I thought my face would split and my heart would burst. Liam twisted round in Mum's arms, and reached for me, so I took him and whirled him round and round.

"Liam! Your daddy's coming home!"

I heard Mum gasp.

"Mum! Everything's going to be all right now," I said, and she laughed, and we all hugged each other. The clouds parted, and sunshine flooded the room, while the noisy corvids cawed, now beneath our window.

Adam was carrying Liam and had his other arm around my waist. I pulled the door to our flat shut when we were all on the landing, turned to face forward, and saw Will, locking his door at the bottom of the first flight of stairs. He'd finally got round to dying his hair. It was a shocking red. He glanced up and saw us, and I watched his heart break. Guilt rushed through me.

"Hi, Will! Long time no see!" I heard Adam say.

Will looked at me. He seemed heartbroken at first, but then his eyes flared with that fire I'd seen in them that day in hospital. He pulled his mouth into a tight smile.

"Kayleigh, I need to show you something," he said, ignoring Adam.

He sounded awful, so I said to Adam, "You boys go on. I'll meet you at the swings in a minute."

Adam pecked me on the lips and carried Liam off down the stairs and out of the building, giving Will a small, awkward smile as he squeezed past.

"What's up, Will?" I asked, lightly, pretending nothing was wrong.

"Why don't you come in?" Will said, sticking the key back in the lock, and twisting it.

His flat was a tip, and I picked my way along the hall, avoiding socks and bits of screwed-up paper.

"Are you okay?" I knew it was a stupid question, but I couldn't stop myself asking it. The vibes coming off him weren't his, and I felt my blood run cold and my eyes start to water. Something was really wrong.

He led me into his work room at the back of the house. I looked out on the beautiful garden automatically, before my gaze fell on a pile of diaries that lay on his desk. 1998 diaries. Cath's novel.

"I thought, while everything else was happening, that I'd read Cath's novel to the end. No-one else seemed bothered about it, not even her best friend," Will said, coldly, watching the guilt flood through me again. He continued, "Not even the police."

"But you said it was unfinished!" I countered. "And the police did read it to the end – well, to where it stopped –"

"There was another diary." Will let the sentence hang in the air. "I didn't give it to them. I was going to burn it, but I just changed my mind."

I was silent.

"There's a letter at the end," Will said, still staring me full in the face. "Not a letter written by Cath, as part of the novel, but an actual letter. One that she found."

I held my breath.

"There's a small scene that ends the novel, and she's just stuck the letter in at the bottom to finish it. Would you like to read it?"

It wasn't a question. I took the letter he had pulled out of the diary he was holding. It was addressed to me, from Adam. I'd never seen it before. My eyes flew over Adam's familiar, spikey handwriting. I looked up at Will, and saw heartbreak, triumph and revenge in his blazing eyes. Then I took the diary, knowing what was coming, and read:

Kayleigh,

Do you remember that night by the pond in Farefield Park? Do you remember that night, Kayleigh? When Cath was in hospital, and we could be free? Run away with me. We said our love would last forever. I can't do this anymore.

Adam

Catherine's Novel

I read the letter I'd found in the CD Lola had returned to me. She obviously had had no idea it was in there, in the with artwork. And the sender of the letter had obviously had no idea that the CD he hid the letter in, wasn't hers. It was an 80s compilation album, and on it was the song, *Kayleigh,* by Marillion. I was numb when I'd read the letter. I couldn't feel a thing. I knew my world had shattered, and that what was left of me had been consumed by Lola's baby, and that I was gone.

I know that I'm going to do it, now. I'll do it in the bath, at Luke's, with the razor blade I nicked from Heath. It'll be violent. I'll have to make the cuts fast and deep. Apparently it's hard to do the second arm, because your slashing hand will be weakened as a result of cutting the first; but I know I'll have the strength. The cuts should be diagonal, too – not straight across. I know I won't feel anything – not the heat of the water, or the throb as the blood leaves my body – because I'm already gone. I'll watch the water redden, and eventually my face will slip under and I will have achieved something, finally.

Epilogue

Dear Dr Farefield,

I received a referral request from HMP Channings Wood today regarding a patient who has been registered to you for many years: a Mr Richard Morrell (NHS no: ___ ___ ___).
It appears that some of the prison officers working in Mr Morrell's block have concerns about his mental state and have therefore asked me to meet with that inmate and make an assessment. Mr Morrell, however, is adamant that no such assessment is required, or that it will, indeed, take place.

I perused his records, but there is no mention of psychiatric disorder.

With this in mind, I am writing to you to ask your opinion on the matter and, in addition, your impression of Mr Morrell's character.

Yours sinc,
Dr E Whittle
Consultant Psychiatrist

Fantastic Books
Great Authors

darkstroke is
an imprint of
Crooked Cat Books

- Gripping Thrillers
- Cosy Mysteries
- Amazing Horrors
- Fascinating Historicals
- Exciting Fantasy
- Young Adult and Children's
  Adventures
- Non-Fiction

Discover us online
www.darkstroke.com

Find us on instagram:
www.instagram.com/darkstrokebooks

Printed in Great Britain
by Amazon